One Life No Sequel

Tomorrows Not Promised

Another
Michael Gainer
Novel

Published by:
Plutonium Publishing, LLC
18520 NW 67th Street Suite 278
Miami, Florida 33015

Library of Congress Control Number: 2003096605

ISBN 0-9714887-1-1
First Printing

Acknowledgements

I'd like to thank my readers for supporting my efforts. I hope you enjoy One Life as much as I enjoyed writing it. I'd also like to thank all the bookstores and book clubs for their support.

1

One

In the final days, there will be many false prophets because so many people are waiting for their savior. But for his part, Kevin believed the only thing that would save him was the dope he was slinging. He had loyal customers: lawyers, doctors, professional athletes, and everyday Joes. Kevin knew he was contributing to their death, but he believed they were killing themselves. After all, he didn't put a gun to their head and make them snort cocaine, smoke crack, pop pills, or shoot up. He figured that some people just liked a glass dick in their mouth.

Kevin thought of himself as an entrepreneur who sold entertainment. The fact that his products had the potential to end lives was an afterthought. Besides, the tobacco industry had been killing folks for years. The only difference between Kevin and them was their address.

"Where them boys at?" a voice called out. It was just another way of asking who had drugs.

"What's up?" Kevin stepped out of the dark alley in

the direction of the voice. His fists were clutched, holding onto his assets.

"Let me get a fifty." Kevin opened his hand and gave the crackhead a fifty-rock of cocaine. Damn junkies, he hated what they did to their families. They got off from work with two weeks of hard-earned cash, then spent their entire check on drugs and ho's. In the meantime, their families were sitting at home in the dark because the electric bill hadn't been paid. How could a man allow his children to wear shitty diapers? Kevin had a real problem with that, but he didn't feel sorry enough for them to quit dealing. He had a family to take care of.

"Where them boys at?"

"Whatcha need, fool?"

"Let me get a dove." The man gave Kevin the money. It took him a minute to unravel the roll of bills.

"Hold up! Say, bitch, this three dollars!" Kevin yelled to the addict. The baser took off in a dead sprint. Looking back to see if Kevin was giving chase, he moved swiftly up the block, running along the buildings.

Kevin pulled out his gun and took aim. The muzzle of his pistol shadowed the baser's every move, no matter how the man ducked, weaved, and bobbed. But Kevin thought otherwise of the mistake he was about to make by blasting that fool. He was selling more birds than a pet shop and he didn't need the cops messing up his hustle. Deciding it was best to deal with that fool later, he knew it was time for him to get off the streets. He was an en-tre-pro-NEGRO who loved having his own money, but the dope game was getting too dangerous.

"Yo G, you shoulda blast that fool." Clyde, Kevin's homeboy, raised his shirt and showed his snub-nosed .357.

Clyde was a "G": a straight gangster. Shoot first, ask questions later. He was one of a few respected between 62nd and 54th Streets, with a reputation for knocking brothers off and knocking brothers out. This nigga was for real. Clyde was the genuine article, the type of cat who would go to your family reunion and slap your grandmother.

The man had had a hard life. He was raised by his grandparents, who died when he was ten. After that he went to live with his mother, who was only eleven years older than he was.

Clyde was a product of an older man taking advantage of a young girl. His father was thirty-five years old when he made Clyde. He'd never met his father--he'd only talked with him on the phone–and Clyde swore to his grandmother before she died that he'd kill his father if he ever met him.

Clyde was only 5'8", but looked like he was chiseled from black marble darker than a thousand midnights. He wore his hair in corn-rows that were always neatly braided and his eyes always had a yellow color that matched his teeth. He wasn't the sharpest knife in the drawer, but he definitely had the biggest balls.

"I'll deal with that dick-sucker later."

"Yo, G, you can't let them basers try you like that! You look bad in front of the boys. You got to deal with that fool so them other basers don't try you. Handle yo' business, buddy. Handle yo' business."

Clyde pimped off down the street slowly, pausing briefly to light his cigarette. He adjusted his pants, which hung way below his waist, and looked back at Kevin, mouthing the words, *handle yo' shit.* Kevin acknowledged, but knew that wasn't his job.

He was the brains of the two-man operation and Clyde was the muscle. Kevin gave Clyde the gift of independence and a piece of his action so that Clyde could eventually start up his own spot. Kevin was a smart street hustler. He understood the business end of the dope game: distribution and fulfillment. But Kevin did not have the muscle it took to hold shit down, and that's where Clyde entered the picture.

Clyde came with a crew of thugs and understood the brutality of the hustle game. Fear will keep a nigga in line when nothing else will. The fear of death, and the loss of limbs and loved ones were his specialties. Kevin noticed the other street hustlers looking at him and shaking their heads. He knew they were thinking that he was getting soft and they wanted his spot. He and Clyde were the only independent hustlers out there. The rest of those clowns worked for someone else. Kevin couldn't see that. At a minimum, his spot pulled in $3K a week and he wasn't about to give the next man $2000 and keep a grand for himself. Shit! He just couldn't see it. As long as Clyde could handle his end of the partnership, the business would survive in spite of small setbacks.

Lately the weather had been real nasty and it looked like it might rain that night. If it did, most of those cats would leave once the sky opened up. But Kevin wasn't going anyplace. It could rain a river. He would just build an ark.

"What they do?" a voice called out from the shadows of the alley. The man came into sight and Kevin focused on the potential customer, staring at the man's feet and looking him over closely before staring him in the eyes.

"What's up, fool?"

"You holding?" The man looked away as he spoke and wiped his nose, sucking up the mucous on his upper lip.

Holding? Holding? What type of question was that? Kevin thought. He said, "I don't serve drugs, officer," and stood there with a smile on his face.

"Shut your mouth, boy! I'll bust your ass right now!" the undercover cop said, standing chest to chest with Kevin. Spit flew as he spoke.

"Do whatcha gotta do, I ain't got nothin' on me," Kevin said, holding his arms out by his side. He knew the cop couldn't pat him down without giving up his identity.

Kevin was cool under pressure. Though he had enough dope on him to get all of Dade County high, he just stood there and looked at the cop with a *what* look on his face.

The cop walked off and Kevin breathed a sign of relief. He was slipping. It was time for him to dip, but before he left . . .

"Five-O, Po-Po in the hole," Kevin yelled as he ran through a wooded area. Them other niggas probably wouldn't have said shit, but he thought he'd save at least one of them from going to jail. He stopped running for a split second and looked back. Those cats where scattering and running around like roaches with the lights on. Kevin saw the cop look back at him, but the guy knew what time it was. He'd need a rocket in his ass to catch Kevin, who hit the corner, went through the alley, and hopped on the bus.

. . . . .

Two buses and a transfer later, Kevin was one block from his crib. He lived in a two-bedroom apartment in Miami Lakes.

"What's up? What's up?" Kevin asked as he entered. "Hey baby, how are you?" Kevin walked into the kitchen, opened the refrigerator, and bit the cap off of a Heineken.

"Everythings cool. Just tryin' to stay away from busters and player haters. I don't know why I came home."

"Man, please." Stephanie was his lady. They'd been

together six years and she was all right. He'd decided she was the one he was going to keep. She was--his ghetto queen.

Stephanie had a caramel-brown complexion and a long, luxurious weave that surpassed her buttocks. She kept a fresh hairdo every week and her gear was always the latest. She only wore the best that Kevin's money could buy. Despite her thick, muscular build, she was very feminine.

She recognized Kevin's strengths as an entrepreneur and knew that one day he would be more than a street hustler. As a matter of fact, she was banking on it. She saw him as the man in the white suit, the one who never got his hands dirty.

"Where's my little man?" The two held each other and swapped spit. Then Kevin grabbed her by the back of the head and licked her on the neck. Stephanie's eyes rolled back in her head as he released her from his grasp.

"He's in the room 'sleep. Don't wake him up!"

"Shit, I'm going to wake him up. My boy needs to see his daddy." Kevin walked towards Ian's room.

"Don't wake him up!" Stephanie grabbed Kevin's arm.

"Why?" he asked, with an agitated look on his face.

"A woman needs to see her man . . . let him 'sleep." Stephanie was hot from their short encounter. She grabbed Kevin's hand and pulled him towards her. Kevin rubbed his hands across her ghetto ass, spreading her cheeks apart. They looked deeply into one another's eyes.

"Make it clap for me, baby." Stephanie pulled slowly away from Kevin. She began to rock from side to side, slowly working her way down to the ground. Then she grabbed her ankles and stood up slowly as she began to gyrate, making her ass clap.

Stephanie was a former stripper, the best in town, and she had mad skills. Her pussy could smoke a cigar and blow out the smoke. She could nearly swallow a beer bottle and she could twist up her body like a pretzel. Kevin often complimented her on her many talents.

POW, POW, POW! Her ass was clapping loud and fast.

"You like that, baby?" She was bent over, holding her ankles.

"You know I do." She continued to dance, making her ass-cheeks jerk one at a time. Then she moved close to Kevin, rubbing his penis.

"Hold on, baby. Let me take a shower. I've been out in these streets all day. I need to wash this filth off me."

"Hurry up! I'm horny. You gonna make me take that dick." Stephanie walked behind Kevin, slapping him on his ass.

"Hold on. I'll be up in ya in a minute."

He took off his work uniform: tennis shoes, socks, oversized sweats, shorts, boxers, a jacket, two shirts of different colors, and a t-shirt. He had to wear all those clothes just in case he had to put them crackers on a high-speed chase.

"Hurry up and take that shit off. You ain't been out there trickin', have you?" Stephanie held his penis in her hands, examining it thoroughly.

"Nah, why you trippin'? Give me my dick back." Kevin jerked his body out of Stephanie's grasp.

"You know I'll know when you cum. That shit better be thick!"

"Whatever. Let me get in the shower."

One thing about having a chick that knew the game: If you slip, she'll grip. Kevin used to let them rock-head women suck him up, but he'd stopped after one of his partners got herpes. He told Kevin that he got sores on his dick just about every three months and that his shit looked like raw hamburger. Whenever he had an episode, he couldn't wear clothes and just sat around, picking at the pus-dripping sores. Kevin swore to himself he was not going out like that.

"Stephanie, count the money. It's in my pocket." Kevin stepped into the shower and turned on the warm water, letting it wash across his face. Then he stood there for a few minutes just to relax as he thought about the day's events.

"Damn!" Stephanie yelled out. Kevin peaked out from behind the shower curtain.

"What's wrong?" he asked. Stephanie was standing there shaking her head and looking at the floor.

"Damn! Look at the shit stains in your drawers. Did you shit on yourself? Make sure you wash yo' ass out. That's a damn shame--a grown-ass man with shit-stained drawers."

"You full of jokes tonight."

"Just wash that ass out," she said, and they both laughed. Kevin was a little embarrassed looking out of the shower at the shitty underwear.

"How much money is it?" He always let her count the money even though he already knew how much it was. His momma didn't raise no fool.

"Baby," Stephanie called to him.

"Yeah," Kevin answered, lathering his face with soap.

"It's $750," she said.

"That's not bad for a day's work. Peel two off for yourself and put the rest up."

"How long before we have enough to buy a house, baby?"

"Not long. Maybe six months or so." Kevin was

hustling dope to buy a home for his family.

"We could get it in three if you let me go back to the club."

"We already talked about that. Do you wanna go back?"

"No, I'm just sayin'."

"Whatcha sayin', huh? Whatcha sayin'?" he yelled loudly, turning off the water.

"Hold it down, you gonna wake the baby." Stephanie said softly, holding one finger to her lips.

"Why you ask me some dumb shit like that? I told you that was a dead issue."

"I just want to help you help us baby, that's all."

"Help me! I don't need no help. The last time you worked the club scene, you got raped. You musta forgot!"

"No, I didn't forget. I'll never forget that. It wasn't my fault. I didn't ask to be raped."

The night of the alleged rape, Stephanie had left the club early to spend time with one of her many men. Kevin wasn't the only hustler in the house. She was out trickin' for extra money and if a customer's cash was right, she would give it up. Only that night, Stephanie's appointment ran a little over schedule.

Kevin was sitting outside the club, blowing up Stephanie's phone. He asked everyone if they had seen her. One of the dancers said she'd gone outside to wait for him. Then Stephanie had pulled into the parking lot and immediately ducked under the dashboard. She told her date to drive past the club and drop her off at the police station.

Stephanie staggered into the station and told the cops she'd just been abducted and raped. They called an ambulance and she was taken to the emergency room. Then the police called Kevin at her request and advised him of the situation. Kevin rushed to her side, angry and unable to forgive himself for not being there in time.

But the entire event was a bullshit hoax by Stephanie, and word got out about her to all the strip-club owners. After that, none of them wanted to take a chance on hiring her crazy ass, despite her many talents.

Stephanie looked up at the ceiling as the tears began to trickle down her face. Then she walked over to the bed and balled up in a fetal position as the tears really began to flow. Kevin walked into the bedroom, drying himself as he spoke.

"Look, I'm sorry. I'm hurt about that situation, too. I shoulda been there." Kevin moved closer to Stephanie. "I'm sorry. Don't cry, baby. Let's just drop it. Let me do this for us. Don't worry, I got this."

Kevin wrapped the towel around his naked body and lay down with Stephanie, holding her in his arms as she cried, and imagined what it must be like to be violated like that. But the worst part was the next day and the day after that. Because after the rape was over, Stephanie had to go on with her life.

Kevin knew it was hard for her. It was hard for him, too, and he prayed every day for the strength to accept it, often asking the Lord to keep Stephanie and his little son strong in case he didn't come home.

Kevin was most concerned about Ian, because Stephanie was a survivor. She had the ability to adapt to any situation at the drop of a hat. Living with her was like living with the seven faces of Eve. Yes, Stephanie would be okay as long as there was a hustle. But despite having two parents seasoned in the game, Ian was uniquely naïve. And that's what worried Kevin most. He squeezed Stephanie softly, kissing her back and apologizing for his outburst.

"Hey Daddy." It was his son. Ian walked in the room

rubbing his eyes. All the commotion had woken him up. "Hey boy, how's Daddy's little man?" Kevin rolled over on his back and looked at his son. Ian climbed in the bed, laying his head on Kevin's chest and hugging him. Then he fell back to sleep. Stephanie on one side, his son on the other.

"Stephanie, are you okay?" Kevin wiped the tears from her face before kissing her on the forehead.

"Yeah, baby, I'm fine."

"I'ma put little man back in his bed." He stood up, carrying his son and looking at his innocent face, when Ian's eyes suddenly opened.

"Hey Daddy." Ian woke up, stretching and straining his eyes.

"Hey boy, I thought you was 'sleep."

"Daddy, you wanna play a game?" He yawned out the words.

"It's late. What kind of game you wanna play?" Kevin asked with a raised brow.

"We'll play a quick game. Okay?"

"Okay, whatcha wanna play?" Kevin gave in reluctantly.

"Cops and robbers. I'll be the cop and you be the robber, Daddy." Kevin put him down and Ian ran to get his badge and handcuffs.

"Let's play another game, son. Daddy don't like that game. I tell you what, little man, how about I read you a bedtime story instead?" Kevin walked down the hall to Ian's bedroom.

"Okay, Daddy."

"Get in the bed." Ian ran and dove in his bed.

"What story do you want me to read?" Kevin thumbed through the many books that lined the bedroom wall.

"I want you to make one up."

"Make up one?" Kevin was surprised.

"Yeah, Daddy."

"Okay, son . . . Once upon a time, there was a man who had a lot of control over many people. He could command their lives effortlessly. And many people believed a man with such power, who looked like he had everything, must be happy and have no troubles. This was a man other men would sell their souls to be. But he had a weakness. Do you know what it was?"

"No, Daddy. What was his weakness?"

"His weakness, son . . . his weakness was himself."

"What made him weak, Daddy?"

"That's a good question. The way he saw himself made him weak. He believed there was value in having power over people and being able to control their lives and the lives of their families. But he realized he had no control over himself. The lesson is that a man--a real man--don't need to control others to be called a man. A man only needs to control himself. Do you understand, son?"

"No, Daddy, I don't."

"You will when you get older, son . . . you will. Now get some rest. I love you. " Kevin kissed his son on the forehead and walked out of the room. Turning off the lights, he stopped and looked back at Ian as he lay in bed, eyes closed, holding his teddy.

Kevin rubbed his head as he walked down the hallway. He knew he was talking about himself. He knew he needed to control himself and stop hustling.

"Stephanie, you 'sleep?" he asked after returning to the dimly lit bedroom. Stephanie was lying on her stomach and her eyes seemed to be closed.

"No, baby. I'm up," she said, rolling over. "Come lay down with me."

Kevin lay down on top of Stephanie and looked at her while he caressed her face, removing the hair that partly covered it.

"I love you. You know that, right?" he asked, looking directly into her eyes.

"Yes, I know. I love you too."

Kevin put his tongue in Stephanie's mouth and began to kiss her slowly and passionately, grinding on her momentarily before moving down to her breast. Then he sucked and nibbled her nipples gently. Stephanie began to moan very softly. Kevin moved down to Stephanie's stomach and stopped at her navel, moving his tongue around slowly inside it. She pushed his head down to her vagina and pulled her legs up to her chest. Kevin put one finger in Stephanie and worked it in circles, pushing in and out at an easy speed. He used his free hand to pull her skin back and expose her clit, licking it once just to tease her. She moaned when his tongue passed across her body. Kevin licked her twice, very slowly, blowing on her vagina before licking her again. Then he removed his finger and replaced it with his tongue. He was in no hurry--he always made Stephanie climax before he entered her. Stephanie's legs began to come down slowly and she raised her head off the bed, watching Kevin eat her.

"Eat it, baby . . . get it." She grabbed his head and rubbed his shoulders, while Kevin moved down to the area between Stephanie's vagina and rectum. That was her spot. Kevin curled his tongue and lapped her up and down, increasing his speed with every lick while Stephanie stimulated herself.

"Baby . . . baby . . . Kevin . . . ummm . . . baby," Stephanie moaned slowly. She had arrived. Kevin moved down her body, kissing her thighs, knees, and calves. Finally, he stuck her toes in his mouth.

"Come get it, baby." Stephanie was beyond ready. Kevin inserted himself slowly in her. Not the whole thing, only the head. He pushed her legs up and rubbed the shaft of his penis between her lips without penetrating her.

"Put it in, baby . . . put it in."

"You want me?"

"Yeah, baby I want you . . . damn, I want you." Kevin put Stephanie's legs down and crawled up on her, never touching her body.

"Take it." Stephanie grabbed his penis and put it in. Kevin lay down on her. He was fully inside and made his penis throb while Stephanie matched his every move. Kevin began to move in and out of her very slowly, kissing her the entire time. The two made love all night.

2

Two

Kevin's days were his nights and his nights were his days. When other families were up and out, he was asleep, locked inside the apartment. A night owl, he didn't get out until the sun went down, unless of course it was the first or fifteenth of the month--or, even better--a holiday. Then he was on the streets "24/7". Once he hustled for seventy-two hours straight and cleared five grand. He had to call Stephanie to come pick up cash twice. *The game can be so sweet*, he thought, *but it's not for everyone. This shit can be tricky*.

It was another night in the dope hole. The sun was going down in the urban jungle and it was showtime, because the freaks came out at night.

"Where them boys at?" a crackhead called out.

"What's up?"

"What's up?" the crackhead replied.

"Bitch, what's up?" Kevin looked him up and down sizing him up.

"Let me get a fifty."

"Haul ass," he said, looking down the street.

"What!"

"You heard me. Haul ass . . . DIP!"

"You ain't tryin' to make this money?" the junkie asked Kevin in disbelief.

"Nah, you keep your money, partna'. Go on to the next man . . . DIP!"

"FUCK YOU!"

"FUCK YO' MAMA! Say something else and I'll bleed you real quiet and leave ya here. Get the fuck on!" The entire time the man was standing there he had his hands in his pockets.

That crackhead didn't want to buy anything. He just wanted Kevin to pull out his stash so he could snatch it and run, but Kevin wasn't falling for the okie-doke. Besides, everybody knew you couldn't catch a crackhead. Buddy didn't want to get cut. All those fools knew Kevin carried a razor and had a reputation for slicing people up.

So the crackhead walked off, looking at Kevin and realizing he'd peeped his game. He'd just have to try and catch one of those other fools slipping.

It was a busy night on the avenue, with a lot of foot traffic. It seemed like all the local junkies wanted to get high, as well as a lot of other people Kevin didn't know.

"Hey baby," A white chick pulled up in an SUV.

"What's up?"

"Come 'ere. I need to talk to you." Kevin walked cautiously over to the truck, mindful that she could be a cop.

"What's up?"

"I need a hit. I need it, baby."

"Whatcha want?" Kevin looked at the truck--then looked down the block.

"I want it all," she said.

"No flow, no dope." He could tell where the

conversation was heading.

"I don't have no money."

"Whatcha got?" As if he didn't know.

"I got some pussy. I'll suck yo' dick. I'll suck yo' friend's dick. I need a hit, baby. Let me suck it, let me fuck you, baby," she said, rubbing her vagina and showing him her breast.

She was fine. She didn't look like a crackhead, but they came in every shape, form, and fashion. She had long red hair with blue-green eyes--the perfect she-devil. "Devil" was the right description because she was a crack monster. If it had been a little later in the night, Kevin would have jumped on that, going into pimp mode to make some money off her. He would have taken her around to all the old pops in the 'hood who couldn't get any pussy and let them hit her--for a small fee, of course. Kevin figured he could probably make a grand off slim and it would only cost him a hundred dollars worth of crack. He reached inside the truck, rubbing her breast and vagina.

"You like the way that feels, baby? You can have it. It's yours."

Just as Kevin was about to change his mind and take her up on her offer, he noticed a little girl in the back seat. She had a terrified and hungry look on her face and Kevin shook his head in disgust.

"Nah, baby girl. I'm straight. Next time." The woman turned around and yelled at the little girl.

"Get down, I told yo' ass to stay down!" She pushed the little girl down onto the floorboard behind the passenger's seat and drove off, moving on to the next man.

Kevin sat back and watched this shit unfold. He knew she was running the same game on the other guy and was curious to see how he was going to react. It took about five minutes for everything to go down and Kevin hated it.

Buddy got in the truck and Kevin hoped for his sake that he knew what he was doing. Kevin also feared for the little girl because he knew her mother was eventually going to pimp her out if she hadn't already.

"Yo money, what's up?"

"What's up?"

"Let me get that dime up outcha."

"I ain't got no dimes . . . twenties or better."

"All I got is a ten."

"That ain't enough."

He walked away from the woman and looked down the block. There he saw one of his best customers rolling up slowly in an LS 430. The guy was principal at one of the local high schools and Kevin greeted him with excitement and respect.

"What's up, playa?" he asked, bending down to the half rolled-up window. A manicured hand, with gold rings on every finger, popped out of the Lexus. Mr. Mendle was an old school player from way back who looked just like "Jerome" from the show, *Martin.*

"What's up? Let me get five," the principal said. This man got high–that was five fifties. The scary shit was that he would be back. Kevin believed he was tricking with high school girls and would be on the ten o'clock news sooner or later, because the brother was starting to look bad. He couldn't possibly hold it together much longer.

"Ah'ight playa, I'll see ya," Kevin told him as the man drove off, rolling up his dark-tinted windows.

It was only eight o'clock and was going to be a good night. Kevin had made about five hundred dollars and it was break-time. He walked across the street to the Arab store to get a sandwich.

"Ahmed, what's up . . . with your magic carpet-flying

ass." He liked fucking with those Arab people. It was all good, because they were hustling too. They were just in different games, but it was the same field.

"Ahmed, don't act like you don't hear me."

"What do you want? Buy something or leave the store."

"Calm down, you camel-riding, turban-wearing, ghetto pimp." Kevin pointed at him and laughed.

"Fuck you, Ready. Buy something or get out." Everyone on the streets knew Kevin as "Ready." He had picked up the name because he was always ready for whatever.

"Ah'ight, calm down!" Kevin leaned over to look at the sandwiches in the glass cooler. "Yeah, let me get that turkey and cheese sub."

"This one?" Ahmed touched the sandwich.

"Nah, the big one, man. The big one. Don't try and give me that li'l shit."

"That's it?"

"Yeah, and let me get this water too." Kevin reached down into a bucket of ice and took out a liter of water. "Damn, that's cold."

"$7.50," said Ahmed.

"$7.50? You trying to rob a nigga?" He gave the attendant his money.

"Keep the change, muthafucka," he said, walking out of the store.

He loved joking with those Arab cats. He didn't fuck around with them too much because they had bust caps in a few niggas around there. They had AK's, AR's, 45's--a fucking arsenal. When you walked in, you might only see two men, but there were ten people in there, all strapped to the teeth. He would fuck with them, but he didn't fuck with them.

"Ready!" a voice called from down the street. He waited for the body to come out of the darkness.

"Who 'dat?" Kevin yelled back.

"It's ya boy, Smitty." Dean Smith, the ex-CEO of a major telecommunications company turned crackhead. This brother had smoked up his job, house, cars, marriage, the kids' college fund, the dog--everything. And still thought he was an important businessman.

Smitty had walked off his job one day and kept walking. That was two years ago and he hadn't changed clothes since. Everyone could tell when he was around because he smelled like rotten meat.

"What they do, Smitty?"

"Ready, my brother, how are things?"

"Yeah, yeah, muthafucka. What?"

"Listen, I need your help, I'm having a slight cash-flow problem. I was wondering if you would be so kind as to spot me a hundred dollars until next week?"

"I don't have a hundred, Smitty," Kevin replied, biting into the sandwich and following it with a gulp of water.

"Oh! I'm sorry to hear that. I guess times are tough all over. Well, if you don't have the money, I'll take some medicine or any drugs you may have." Smitty extended his hand.

"You funny, Smitty. Funny as hell. I can't help you, brother, spread yo' hustle." Kevin nearly choked from laughing.

"Thank you for your time, Mr. Ready. I'll be speaking with you soon." Smitty buttoned his weather-beaten overcoat, saluted Kevin, and walked down the block.

Kevin knew crack was a beast. He thought about how everyone used to look up to Dean. He himself had once admired the man and aspired to be like him because Dean was the smartest kid in school, the best athlete, and the type of guy your sister would marry. You couldn't help but love him. He went to college and graduated summa cm laude and repeated with the same honors from graduate school.

Smitty was a local celebrity. He had landed the bomb job in his hometown and married a woman who was amazing. Smitty's wife wasn't a dime--she was more like a quarter. Smitty had had it all until he sucked on that glass dick.

Kevin felt a little responsible for Smitty's fall from the mountain top because he had sold him his first hit. First, Smitty had rolled the crack in cigarettes and weed. Then he graduated into a full-blown crackhead within a few short months. Kevin had that effect on most people he knew. He witnessed the effects of the beast first-hand. His hero, Smitty, had become a baser. Life was crazy.
He walked back to his spot and posted up, ready to make his money.

"What's up, baby?" It was Monica, one of his old chicken-heads.

Monica was a slim red-bone from Ft. Lauderdale with autumn-brown eyes and shoulder-length hair dyed honey-blond. In a nutshell, she was five-foot-five and bow-legged, with an ass like a midget.

She depended on the first and fifteenth like other people depend on air. Her entire life was WIC checks, Section 8, and EBT. And she also had a hustle on the side as a professional booster. If given the chance she would steal the taste out of your mouth. The trunk of her Impala stayed full of the best that southern Florida's retail industry had to offer. All of the shit was hot. She nearly cleaned Bal Harbor out, and Thursday through Saturday she would get her hustle on, visiting local hair salons and selling her products. She was making a killing, living "ghetto fabulous."

"What's up, slim?" Kevin asked Monica.

"I've missed you. You don't return my beeps when I call."

"Well, you know I'm on my job, making this money."

"You can still give a sister a call. I just wanna give you some, that's all."

"That's all, huh?"

"Yeah, that used to be enough."

Kevin bent over and leaned in the car, looking at her fat pussy bulging through her shorts. That thing was so fat it looked like a pile of dirty clothes. *Most women have a V-print*, he thought, but when he looked down at Monica, she had a W. That monkey was fat.

"What's up? What's up right now?" he asked, rubbing her vagina.

"Get in," she said as she grabbed his hand and pushed it hard against her. He paused for a moment as he watched her rubbing her cat. She was creaming; he could feel the moisture through her shorts.

"Get in," she said again in a soft, yearning voice. He walked around the car, opened the door, and sat down.

"Where to?" Monica asked.

"Pull around behind the store." Kevin pointed to the alley and Monica drove slowly around to the back of the store.

"Behind the store! What happened to the hotel?"

"I ain't got time for that." He looked at her with a raised brow. "What's up? You want this or what?" Kevin opened the door as if he were about to get out of the car.

"You gotta rubber?" She smacked her teeth and looked out the window.

"Yeah." Kevin smirked slightly before closing the

door. He took the rubber out of his jacket and opened it as she pulled down his sweats. Then he put the condom on the dashboard and helped Monica pull down his layers of clothes.

"Give it to me." She took the condom from the dashboard and put it into her mouth, grabbing his penis and jacking it softly. Then she bent down and put him in her mouth.

"Suck it baby, suck it." She was sucking it good. He could feel her slobber running down his balls. Monica was known for sucking the color out of brothers.

HUM, HUM, HUM. Monica was humming and making her jaws vibrate. When she sat up and wiped the slobber from her chin, Kevin looked down and the rubber was on.

"You ready for this pussy now?"

"Yeah, take ya shorts off." Monica leaned back in the seat and raised her hips to wiggle out of her skin-tight shorts. She had the fattest, hairiest cat on the planet. Kevin pushed her softly down onto the seat and climbed on top of her. Monica opened her legs wide, hanging one over the seat and pushing the other off the windshield. She grabbed Kevin and put him inside her. Right out the gate Kevin was banging her hard and fast. He was wide open, up and down, in and out.

"You like it?" Kevin humped, increasing his speed with each stroke.

"I love it," she said, howling out the words. He had her squealing like a pig. Kevin raised himself up and looked at Monica. He enjoyed watching his penis go in and out of her.

Monica grabbed Kevin by the ass and pulled him to her and then away. She was banging him just as hard as he was banging her. With his every downward motion she met him half-way, raising up off the seat.

“Ahh, ahh! You making me cum.” He started going faster and harder. Then Kevin came hard and could feel the semen leaving his body in rapid gushes. Monica lay back and let him get it! It felt like a water balloon bursting on concrete. And that’s just about what it was like, because they had a problem.

“Oh shit!” he said in a loathing voice.

“What happen? What’s wrong?” Monica asked, huffing out the words.

“The condom broke.”

“Broke? The condom broke? Ready, I know you didn’t cum in me. Tell me you didn’t nut in me.”

“I came in you. The cum is in you. The rubber broke. What was I supposed to do?”

“Take it out, take it out. You know how my pussy feel without a rubber.” She grabbed his dick to make sure the rubber was torn.

“Fuck that. All I know is, I hope you ain’t burning.” Kevin removed the remaining part of the condom from the base of his penis.

“Burning? Ready, I know you just didn’t try me like some ho’!” Monica inserted her finger in her vagina, trying to find the remaining piece of rubber.

“You a ho’. You just got fucked in yo’ car, behind the store, in the dope hole. You a ho’.”

“Fuck you, Ready!” Monica located the broken condom and threw it out the window.

“You just did . . . don’t be mad at me ’cause the rubber broke. You need to shave that hairy-ass pussy you got.” Kevin pulled up his clothes.

“If I’m pregnant I’m going to keep the baby.”

“Bitch . . . is you crazy?”

“Yeah, I’ll be yo’ bitch!” Monica grabbed the end of Kevin’s shirt and wiped her cum-smeared vagina.

"We'll see. Let me out this muthafucka. Oh yeah, by the way, thanks for the fuck." Kevin sarcastically muttered, leaving the car. He walked back over to his spot, thinking he'd probably missed about two hundred dollars, when he was quickly rushed by a known client.

"Ready."

"What's up?"

"Let me get a twenty." He made the exchange and moved on, angry that he'd wasted so much time.

"Ready!" It was Monica, the freak he'd just screwed.

"What?" he yelled, throwing his hands into the air.

"I'll see yo' punk ass in nine months!"

"WHATEVER, BITCH!" he yelled, while Monica sped off down the street leaving a trail of smoke.

Kevin knew he'd made a mistake. *Dumb-ass me,* he thought. He'd had enough of these streets. It was time to take it to the house.

. . . . .

But Kevin wasn't the only one tricking that night. Stephanie had her man over to their apartment.

"Hey baby." The two kissed.

"What's up, baby girl? Is Ian 'sleep?"

"Yeah, he's asleep. Come on in." The man was leery about being in Kevin's house.

"What are you looking around for? Relax, everything's cool."

"You call your boy?"

"No, not yet." Stephanie picked up the phone and dialed Kevin's cell number. The phone rang a few times before he answered.

"What's up, baby?" Kevin asked, recognizing the number on the caller ID.

"Hey baby, I was just calling to say I miss you." Stephanie said to Kevin while she unzipped the man's pants. "You still on the set?"

"Yeah, but I'm about to get up out of here. I'll be home in about an hour."

"Okay baby, see you when you get home."

"Ah'ight, see you soon."

Stephanie hung up the phone and dropped the silk robe that adorned her body. She led the man by the hand as they walked softly past Ian's room, careful not to wake him.

"Take this shit off," Stephanie said, helping to take off the man's clothes. She dropped to her knees and gave him head.

"Ahhh." His loud moaning was drowned out by her slurping on his penis.

"Get in bed." Stephanie pushed the man down onto the mattress and put his penis inside her. She turned around with her ass facing him and did a split. Then she squeezed her vaginal muscles before she began to fuck the shit out of him.

"Damn, you can fuck." The man paused as he watched her work. "Damn, this pussy good."

Stephanie turned and faced him. She stood on her feet without removing the man from inside her and held her knees, popping and grinding.

"Don't cum in me. Let me know when you're cuming. I wanna suck it out."

"I'm about to nut, baby." Stephanie hopped off the man just as the semen was spewing and put him in her mouth, sucking and swallowing. He moaned like a bitch, inching away from her, but there was no escaping: She had engulfed his entire penis and balls. She cleaned him up real good before releasing him from her mouth.

"Damn, girl, you good. I'ma hate to give you up." Stephanie looked up, wiping the corners of her mouth.

"Whatcha mean, give me up?"

"This shit is getting too crazy. Me coming over here . . . Ian is ten feet away. Shit, Kevin could walk in at anytime and kill us both."

"So what you supposed to be, breaking up with me?"

"Yeah, I guess that's what I'm doing."

"You fuck me . . . cum in my mouth . . . then tell me we're through! You got me fucked up." The man got out of bed and quickly began putting on his clothes and shoes.

"Girl, you all loud and shit. You about to wake up that boy."

"How you fuck my face one minute and dump me the next?"

"See, this is why we just need to end this shit. It's too crazy. I can't be caught up in no shit like this."

"You already caught up. Bitch, you belong to me."

"No I don't. It's over."

"Get yo' shit and get the fuck up out my house." The man hurried through the apartment, pulling his shirt over his head, while Stephanie picked her robe up off the floor and put it on. "Bitch, this shit ain't over. I'ma get you fucked up."

"Whatever."

"Get the fuck up out my shit." The man walked out of the apartment and Stephanie slammed the door behind him. Ian emerged from his bedroom rubbing his eyes.

"Momma, is everything okay?"

"Everything's fine. Go back to bed." Stephanie kissed the boy and sent him back to his room.

3

Three

You can see some really weird shit at the bus stop, Kevin thought. Strange-looking, bizarre people ride the bus. But this was Miami, where strange was the norm.

He waited at the stop at the corner of 27th Avenue and 79th Street, and pretended not to notice the girl standing next to him. She had on a white, chiffon dress that was completely see-through, from head to toe. And under it she had on a bright turquoise bra and matching underwear. As he tried hard not to stare at her body, he noticed her shoes, which were turquoise like her undergarments. Apparently she tried to coordinate her underwear with her shoes. Plus she had on an electric-blue Lil' Kim wig to match. Kevin thought *she must be high, waiting on 79th Street with neon panties on.* Then he remembered that it was 79th Street and she was working.

"Excuse me, sir. Can you tell me how to get to Hollywood Boulevard?" a man asked Kevin.

"You a long way from there. That's all the way in

Broward County. Fool, you in Dade."

"I have a doctor's appointment and I need to get there. Can I borrow some coins to catch the bus?" Kevin thought, *that fool knows the Metro bus don't go to Broward. Besides, what doctor's office is open at this time of night? He just trying to hustle up some change to buy some crack.* Kevin looked down at him with a smirk on his face.

"I ain't got no change, partna'."

"Come on, brother. Let me get a penny, quarter, dollar--something."

"I ain't got it. Haul ass. Spread yo' weak-ass hustle."

Kevin looked down the street and saw the bus approaching. He threw his hand out, signaling it to stop, as he pulled out sixty cents for the ride.

"I thought you didn't have no change," the crackhead said.

"I ain't say I ain't have no change. I just ain't got no change for yo' ass." Kevin got on the bus, paid the fare and walked toward the back, eyeballing everyone he passed to make sure that no one he was looking for was on it. Then he noticed one man and stopped and stared at him because the guy's face looked familiar.

"Where I know you from, fool?"

"You don't know me, playa." The man looked out the window as he spoke.

"My bad, I thought I knew you." Kevin walked off toward the back of the bus, rubbing his chin. He felt a little uneasy because he didn't know if he'd misused the man in some way.

Kevin made it a habit to sit in the back of the bus because he preferred to keep everyone in front of him. He sat down and began searching his thoughts. He knew he'd seen that cat before. And suddenly he remembered. The bus came to a stop and the stranger got off. Even though it was not Kevin's stop, he got off too.

"Yo, playa . . . yo!" The stranger walked on, acting like he couldn't hear Kevin. But Kevin quickly ran up beside him.

"Yo, playa . . . what's up?" And before the stranger could speak, Kevin punched him in the mouth, following the haymaker up with a three-piece combo. Two to the head and one to the body. The stranger fell to the ground clutching his face, and blood flowed between his fingers.

"Why you doing this . . . why?"

"Shut up!" Kevin kicked buddy in the stomach.

"You snatched some dope from me last week!" Kevin muttered in an aggressive voice, kicking the man repeatedly. The guy tried to scurry away but the size twelve Timberland would not allow him to escape. Kevin walked slowly behind the man, kicking him hard every few steps.

"I'm sorry, I won't do it again. I'm sorry."

The more he begged and cried, the more furious Kevin became and, kneeling down, he punched him repeatedly in the face until he had beaten the man unconscious. Then he ran off, leaving the guy un-responsive and bleeding. He didn't know if he was dead or alive. Kevin ran four blocks before he stopped at a laundromat, and from there he called a cab. As he walked to the sink to wash the blood off his knuckles, he snarled at everyone, but they appeared not to notice him. There are certain rules in the city and "Mind your own business" is rule #1.

At home that night Kevin watched the news to see if any murders were reported, and was pleased to see that there were none. That was good, but he had to represent on that fool--he just had to. He felt like he'd just handled his business, and if the man died, he died. Kevin wasn't about lose any sleep over it. That baser chose his destiny when he stole from him.

.....

The next morning when Kevin woke up he looked at his bruised knuckles and recalled the way he had savagely beat the man. He also remembered the little girl in the truck. And then he thought about Dean Smith. His life began to flash before his eyes. He wasn't doing dope, but the dope game was his life and he needed a way to break free. This was a business that didn't require a conscious. Maybe it was time for him to get out of the game and be a role model to his son. Kevin didn't know how to do it, but he had an idea.

"Stephanie, are there any churches around here?"

"Yeah, a few. Why?" Stephanie stood in the doorway looking at Kevin inquisitively as she massaged Kemi Oil through her weave.

"Get little man dressed."

"Why?'"

"We're going to church!" Kevin said with excitement.

"Church? Church?" Stephanie replied with a bewildered look on her face.

"Ready, you don't own a suit, let alone a tie."

"You don't need a suit to go to church. I'm going to

listen to the word of the Lord. I don't need a suit, all I need is Jesus."

"Preach on, brother, preach on!" Stephanie screamed, as she did a Holy Ghost shuffle. "I'll get Ian ready. I'm so excited, baby. We do need the Lord in our lives, we do. What made you wanna go to church?"

"I don't know, a lot of different things. I'm living foul. Moreover, this family is living foul. We need some guidance and direction other than what's on the street."

"I feel you, baby. Give me about an hour." Stephanie ran through the apartment excitedly, looking for something to wear.

"Now what should I wear?" Kevin was talking to himself. Stephanie was right: he didn't own a suit or a tie. He didn't even have a button-up shirt. "That's all right, I'll just put on these gold silk slacks and this cream and gold Ferragamo shirt. With these matching 'gators . . . of course. If I'm going to the House of the Lord, I might as well go looking good."

Stephanie walked into the room, falling to her knees as she pointed and laughed.

"I know you not wearing that!" She laughed hysterically between each spoken word.

"Why not? This some good shit. You know how much this shit cost?" Kevin held the clothes against his naked body as he looked in the mirror.

"Yeah baby, you right. This shit is fly. It's nice for the club, but not church," Stephanie explained as she rubbed the silky material against Kevin's chest. "Honey, you don't wear Ferragamo to church."

"Why not?" Kevin asked with a puzzled look.

"Because, silly, you look like a drug dealer. Besides, I'm with you and you ain't about to be looking crazy walking with me."

"So what you saying is . . . I'll look like a drug dealer if I wear this, right?" Stephanie nodded her head. "But you with me, so what that make you look like? Wait, let me answer that . . . a stripper?" Stephanie looked at Kevin with tear-filled eyes.

"Why do you always say stuff to hurt me, Kevin?"

"I didn't mean to hurt you. It just seemed like you were putting me down, talking about my clothes. These are the only types of clothes I got. See, this' why we need the Lord in our life. I hurt you and I don't even know it." Kevin knew damn well what he was doing, but the shit sounded so good. "Maybe going to church will help me. I hope it gives me the strength I need to change. Not for you or Ian, but for me." Stephanie wiped the tears from her face.

"I feel you, baby. Let's get ready and go."

Kevin turned back to the mirror and held up the outfit he'd selected. His clothes may not have been appropriate, but they were all he had other than street clothes, so he decided to wear what he had. It was the best he could do. Not to mention the fact that the Ferragamo shirt cost $1,500.00. That was five cheap suits put together.

"Stephanie, what are you wearing?"

"I'm wearing my red dress with my red Gucci stilettos."

"For real?"

"Nah, man, I'm just kidding. I'll probably wear a blue or yellow dress, something very subtle."

"You don't have nothing in gold? I want us to match, so put Ian on something gold too."

Kevin knew Stephanie didn't want them to dress alike. But he thought it would be cool if they looked like a family. Family was important to him and he hoped Stephanie felt the same way.

"Okay, baby, we'll all wear gold."

"Cool. I'll be ready in about forty-five minutes."

4

Four

Kevin was glad he'd had the car detailed the day before. His auto was phat--a candy-red, 1974, box Chevy with tan leather seats that sat on twenty-three-inch rims. It had fifteen-inch woofers with two thousand-watt amps, and that get-down was in the trunk.

"Kevin, don't turn on the music." Stephanie said with a stern look on her face.

"I don't even want you to think about it. Don't roll up to the church booming."

"I got a little sense. Give a brother some credit. I'll crank my shit after church." Kevin turned off the system. "You look real nice, baby. It's been a long time since I've seen you in a dress." Kevin paused at the red light and looked at Stephanie. He'd forgotten how beautiful she really was.

"Why are you looking at me like that?" She blushed.

"'Cause I like the way you look, and you smell good too." He caressed her face and winked his eye.

"Thank you, you make me feel pretty." Kevin looked in the rearview mirror at his little son, who was looking back at him.

"Daddy."

"Yes, son?"

"Where are we going?"

"We're going to church."

"What's a church?" Kevin stumbled. He wasn't sure how to answer his son. He knew he wasn't an ideal role model for his child but he wanted him to have the Lord in his life. What Kevin was about to say and how Ian experienced it would be his foundation as it pertained to church and religion. So Kevin thought, *What should I say?*

"Church is a place where people go to worship the Lord and give thanks for being alive," Stephanie explained to their son, seeing the uncertainty on Kevin's face. He reached over and touched her on the thigh to thank her for interceding. She grabbed his hand and smiled.

"Turn here. There's a church at the end of the street--St. Joseph Baptist Church. My grandmother was a member of it when she was alive. We had her funeral there too." Stephanie held her head down.

"Are you sure you wanna go to this church? We can find another one if you want." Kevin placed his hand on Stephanie's back, rubbing her gently.

"No, I'm fine. I just miss Nanna, that's all. She was the only person besides you and the baby who ever cared about me."

"It's ah'ight, baby girl. I love you, and little man loves you too."

"I know. I'm fine, baby. This is a good church. I'm fine." They pulled up to the church. It was huge--a house of glass. The House of the Lord. It was so packed that Kevin had to park down the street because the parking lot was full.

"Come on, guys, let's go." He was eager to start his

new life as a churchgoer.

"Are we here, Daddy? Is this the church?" Ian looked at the massive building.

"Yes, son. We're here. This is church."

Kevin, Stephanie, and Ian walked up to the front door. Kevin held Stephanie next to him with his left arm and carried his son in his right. He was afraid and could feel his heart pounding like it was about to explode.

"I hope they got AC in here. I ain't with holding one of those fans," he said jokingly to ease the tension.

"Boy, you know you crazy." Stephanie kissed Kevin on the cheek.

When they walked into the church they were immediately ushered to the back corner of the balcony.

"Excuse me, man. I don't want to sit up here. I want to sit downstairs, up in the front. I see a few empty spots," Kevin said softly into the usher's ear, pointing to the front of the church.

"I'm sorry, sir, but all those seats are reserved for members of the church."

"I thought this was the House of the Lord. I didn't know you had to be a member to sit down front." Stephanie squeezed Kevin's hand tightly--his cue to chill out.

Kevin looked around at the people in the pew and they looked like a sea of uptown Negroes. Everyone had their noses turned up. He didn't say anything else. He had come for one purpose and one purpose only. Leaning over to Stephanie, he whispered, "Ain't this a bitch. They acting like they better than us."

"No they're not. You're over-reacting. Just sit back and listen to the sermon, and don't curse in church."

"I'll sit back and I'll listen, but I know how I feel." Kevin had his lip turned up, revealing his gold teeth.

The choir began to sing and the sounds were

heavenly. All the tension Kevin felt immediately left him. Stephanie sang along and Ian was singing too. He didn't know the words but it didn't matter because he was rejoicing at what he heard.

Then, while the choir sang, a man came out who was dressed in an all-white silk robe with gold trim. Kevin leaned over to Stephanie and asked, "Who is that?" She told him he was the reverend of the church, Reverend Johnson.

Reverend John Johnson was a neighborhood kid and the son of the pastor who founded St. Joseph Church. He had grown up in the streets of Liberty City and, as a child, he'd been called "PK" since he was the preacher's kid. He was always trying to prove himself to his peers while remaining a preacher's son. He couldn't wait to grow up so he could get out from under the watchful eye of his father and the community.

Later, when he moved to New York for three years, no one really knew what he did there. His family never heard from him, but it was rumored that the good reverend was a major player, hustling in the streets of Harlem and Brooklyn. Eventually, his country ass fucked over some people and he had to run back home. Some even believed that the only reason he took over his father's church was to gain some security from the Asian mobster-types who were trying to kill him. They say all you need to start a church is a nigga with game and two faithful ho's, and you can pimp the flock. A reverend could be on the path of gaining the world, but could lose his soul in the process.

Kevin was shocked. He was expecting some old dude to come out, but this brother was about his age. Kevin had never seen a preacher that young before.

But then, Reverend Johnson was not a typical pastor. He was coal-black with hazel eyes. Not muscular, but very fit, he was neither tall nor short, and had perfectly straight teeth that were white as snow. A diamond cross dangled from his left ear and he had a very unusual hairstyle: He wore finger-waves that were more like ocean waves. In fact, the parishioners often joked that they'd get seasick if they looked at his hair too long.

All of the reverend's clothes were tailor-made. He wore his slacks high around his waist and tight in the crotch because he thought it made him look like James Brown when he did the Holy Ghost shuffle. And all of his style was accented by a five-carat pinky ring that matched the diamond bezel on his Rolex watch.

He walked up to the pulpit, raised his hands above his head, and began to bring them down slowly. As they descended the choir began to sing softer and softer, and by the time his hands were at his sides, the choir was humming. The entire scene was absolutely astonishing--better than something on television.

Then the reverend opened his mouth and Kevin would never forget what he said: "In all thy ways acknowledge him." That was a very powerful statement and Kevin knew it would change his life. He thought it meant that no matter what you do, give all the praise to God.

Then the reverend began to preach.

"Good morning, church." The church replied in all different voices, "Good morning, Reverend."

"The Lord is good. I wanted to share that with you today." Then he repeated it in a louder and more emphatic voice: "The Lord is good." People in the church amen'd, well now'ed, and replied, "all the time."

"God is good! Why then is there so much evil in the world? I want you to answer that question for me, church. Why is there so much evil in the world?"

At that very moment Kevin went into a trance. He

got a blank stare on his face and he didn't hear anything the reverend said after that. His mind began racing and he ran the question through his head over and over again, searching for an answer. God is good, so why is there so much evil in the world? What role does the devil play in this evil? What makes us do evil things?

Kevin thought, *I deal drugs, but I deal to support my family. If I didn't persevere we wouldn't eat. Am I evil?* No matter how hard he tried he just couldn't shake any of those questions from his thoughts, and he began to see his life like a movie. The hustling, the pimping, and his daily life on the streets. He thought, *Damn,maybe I am a monster. In saving my family, I'm killing the next man's dream.*

An hour had passed and the collection plate was being passed.

"Kevin . . . Kevin. Whatcha doing, daydreaming?" Stephanie touched him on the arm.

Kevin reached for the collection plate and took it from Stephanie.

"Do you think I'm evil?" he asked her.

"What?"

"Do you think I'm evil?"

"No, I don't think you're evil. I think you trippin'. Are you feeling okay?" She placed her hand against his forehead.

"Yeah, I'm feeling good. I'm okay, I guess. I just have some questions in my head I need answered."

"Okay, baby. But before you answer those questions put some money in the plate. I think the usher wants it back." Stephanie looked up at the usher and gave him a quick smirk.

"Oh . . . my bad. How much should I put in?"

"A hundred dollars is good."

The young boy's eyes almost popped out of his head

as Kevin peeled a hundred-dollar bill off a roll fat enough to choke a goat. He placed the bill in the plate and passed it back to the usher.

The choir began to sing again and Kevin had never heard the sounds of angels, but he was sure they were heavenly. Then the reverend asked all visitors to please stand up, but Stephanie was reluctant to stand. She stood up slowly and looked down at Ian.

Kevin couldn't see the downstairs of the church because they were so far in the back. All he saw was the reverend staring at him. Well, it seemed like he was staring at him. Then, after the reverend had welcomed all the visitors to the church, he asked everyone to be seated.

"Church, the Lord works in mysterious ways." Reverend Johnson said, just before bending down to whisper into an usher's ear. About five minutes passed before Kevin was tapped on the shoulder.

"Excuse me, sir. We have some seats down in the front. Would you and your family like to move?"

"Sure," Kevin said eagerly. "Sure, we'd love to move downstairs." He felt like they were George and Louise, moving on up.

The usher seated them about five rows back from the pulpit. And while Kevin walked through the huge church he took in all the sights. He noticed the architectural genius it must have taken to construct the building, which was beautiful. And he looked at all the church members' faces as he passed each row. Some of them were elbowing the person next to them, signaling them to look. Yeah, they were looking at Kevin and his family, but Kevin recognized some of them too. A few were raising their hymnals to cover their faces but they didn't have to worry because their secret was safe with him.

"Why do you think they moved us?" Kevin asked

Stephanie.

"I don't know." Stephanie shrugged her shoulders.

The reverend walked back to the pulpit and raised his arms above his head as he looked up at the ceiling with closed eyes. Then he began to drop his arms slowly as he opened his eyes and the choir sang more and more softly until they were only humming the hymn.

"In all thy ways acknowledge him. Church, we have some new people amongst us this morning." Kevin's heart began beating fast. He didn't know who else was new to the church but he knew it was their first visit and he grabbed Stephanie's hand as she slid closer towards him. Then he picked Ian up and sat him on his lap as the preacher went on to say, "Amongst the righteous will walk the unrighteous, the unholy, those that are not God-like--those who are sinners. You should not socialize or verbalize with these individuals, for they are sent to do the devil's work." He paused to wipe his forehead. "The devil is bold and his workers may even visit the House of the Lord. We must be cautious not to be led astray by these ungodly types."

Kevin felt he was talking about him. And the reverend *was* talking about Kevin. That's why the ushers had brought him and his family down from the balcony. Kevin felt he was the monkey the reverend was using to promote his show.

Everyone in the church was amening his every word, but what he was saying was not true, at least not about Kevin. Kevin didn't know much about the Lord but he had been taught that the Lord knows your heart and he felt his heart was is in the right place. And he had not come to church to be belittled, degraded, or embarrassed in front of his son and Stephanie. He was glad Ian was asleep. Then Stephanie leaned over to him and said, "Kevin, I'm ready to go. Let's go. Let's go, baby."

"Okay." They stood up to walk out of the church and saw that the people had a distinct look of hate on their faces, like they were looking at Satan himself. Kevin knew this wasn't the House of the Lord, at least not his Lord.

On their way out the reverend added, "Do you see? God is good, and evil has no place in our church." He said it all in reference to Kevin and his family.

Kevin guessed he was an easy target because of the way he was dressed. He knew he looked like a drug dealer or a pimp. So even though he thought he should maybe be mad at the reverend, he wasn't. He figured the guy had just done what he felt was right.

On their way home, they were quiet. Kevin didn't say anything about what had happened and neither did Stephanie. It was a bad experience and they decided to leave it at that. But as the church began to fade in the rearview mirror, the questions that seemed to haunt Kevin invaded his thoughts again. *I deal drugs, but I deal to support my family. Am I evil?* Kevin still had those questions in his head and they needed to be answered.

Later, Stephanie told Kevin that the reverend wanted her to be his lady, and went on to explain that he'd come to the strip-club to watch her dance. Kevin remembered that the Bible says that there will be many false prophets in the last days, and he just hoped that Reverend Johnson didn't lead his flock into the very abyss he claimed to be saving them from.

5

Five

Kevin awoke before dawn the next day, after a restless night. He was still fuming over Sunday's events because he had just tried to do the right thing by taking his family to church. And all night he'd questioned himself, wanting to know if the Lord had singled him out and used the reverend to send him a message. When he did drift off, he only saw the reverend taunting him.

Sitting up in bed, Kevin watched the room slowly illuminate from the rising of the morning sun. Monday was the day he usually took off. Mondays, Tuesdays, and Wednesdays were notoriously slow and dangerous because the jump-outs rode on those days and if you wanted to go to jail, they were the best days for it to happen. No matter how badly Kevin needed money, he would not hustle on those days.

But hustling was the last thing on his mind this Monday, because Kevin had more pressing matters to deal with. Three hours passed and he still hadn't moved.

Stephanie had gotten up and was moving around

the apartment. She knew that Kevin wasn't in a good mood and she always kept her distance at times like that. When she came into the bedroom and turned on the television, she was accompanied by Ian, who stood next to Kevin.

"Steph . . . you know that punk-ass reverend really tried me. He disrespected me in the presence of my woman and my son, not to mention the entire church. My own flesh and blood, flesh of my flesh."

Kevin was furious as he thought about the embarrassment he and his family had endured. "I made my mind up," he said, looking down at Ian and rubbing the top of his boy's head.

"Made up yo' mind about what?"

"I got to deal with buddy. He's fuckin' with the wrong . . ."

"Hold on, don't do anything you'll regret later. If something happens to you, then what? Who will take care of your son? What about us?" She put her hands on Kevin's face and looked him directly in the eyes as she spoke.

"I can't let that ride. I can't! Buddy tried me. I think he still likes you or something. What happened? You fucked him, or did he fuck you over? What happened, Steph?"

"Don't get mad at me because of what happened yesterday. I didn't know that was gonna happen. If I did, we woulda gone someplace else."

"Something about that whole scene smells fishy to me. I don't know what it is, but I'ma find out."

"Whatcha gon' do, Kevin, huh? Get Clyde to handle yo' business? You know whenever he get involved, something stupid go down. Whatcha gon' do, Kevin? Or should I call you 'Ready', 'cause now you ready for whatever."

"That's right. I'm Ready. Ready for whatever, and I'm not about to let that fool slide."

Kevin was in a trance and sat on the end of the bed, lacing up his boots. He slid on a wife-beater and was ready to handle his business. The entire time he was getting dressed, he plotted the reverend's demise. *Should I burn the church down? No, that's no good. They probably have insurance. They'll just rebuild a bigger, better church. Maybe slap his punk ass in the back of the head with a nine double m. That should straighten his ass out. No, that's not painful enough.*

"So your boy used to come to the club?" Kevin rubbed his chin as he questioned Stephanie.

"Yes, Kevin. Why?"

"I just know how I'ma get him." Kevin shook his head up and down, confirming all his thoughts.

"Kevin, just let it go. Let it go, baby."

"I ain't lettin' shit go. You can bet that on my unborn seeds." Kevin stood up, moving Stephanie to the side as he walked out of the room.

"Where in the fuck are you going, Kevin?"

"Out! It's on."

Kevin drove up to the church and circled the block, checking out the church grounds. Then he drove through the huge gate and into the empty parking lot. The only car was a pearl Cadillac in the spot marked "Pastor - St. Joseph Church."

There was an older man on the grounds raking leaves. Kevin pulled up, threw his car into park, and looked around, checking out the surroundings. Then he got out of the car and approached the man slowly.

"Excuse me, sir," he said. "Can you tell me where I might find Reverend Johnson?"

"Sure, young man. The good Reverend Johnson is in his office in the church. He just went inside about ten minutes ago."

"Thank you." Kevin moved towards the church entrance. "One more thing. Can you let me in?"

"The church isn't closed, son. It's always open."

"Thanks again."

Kevin walked up to the church doors, swinging them open as he walked inside. He paused momentarily as yesterday's entire encounter ran through his mind. Although the church was empty, he could still hear the snickering and comments of the parishioners. Breathing hard and fast, he walked down the aisle that twenty-four hours earlier he had rushed out of.

"Reverend!" Kevin yelled out. "Reverend Johnson!" Kevin's voice echoed through the empty building.

"Yes, who is it?" The reverend emerged from a small room in the back of the church.

"It's Kevin Gray."

"Kevin Gray. I'm sorry, but that name escapes me." Kevin walked a little closer so he could see his face.

"Remember me now?"

"Oh yeah." The Reverend looked Kevin up and down. "You were here yesterday with Stephanie. Of course I remember you. So the sinner returns." The reverend turned his back and walked towards his office.

"Don't turn your back on me, punk!" Kevin grabbed his shoulder and spun him around.

"Listen, boy, you ain't on the street and don't let this white collar fool you. I'm from the projects. It can be however you want it to be." The pastor clutched his teeth and bawled his fist. He looked like Barney Fife trying to play hard, and Kevin almost wanted to laugh. The reverend wasn't from the projects. It was more like he was from *around* the projects. His family only lived in Liberty City because it looked good. That "*we all on same level*" type of thinking. The reverend definitely had the softest hands in the ghetto.

"What, is that the toughest thing you can say? Be glad you got that white collar on your neck. Otherwise I'll be up in yo' . . ."

"Silence, don't use profanity in the House of the Lord!" he yelled, stepping towards Kevin.

"Who you talking to? You think you talking to one of your faithful followers? I ain't got no love for ya, playa, and you gon' get dealt with before it's all said and done." Kevin grilled the pastor and showed him all sixteen gold teeth.

"Is that a threat?"

"Take it how I said it!"

"I knew this day would come," the reverend said with released emotion.

"What do you mean, you knew this day would come?" Kevin turned and tilted his head to the side, trying to make sense of the reverend's statement.

"Ask Stephanie. She'll explain. But right now is not the time or place . . . you be careful."

"Why?"

"I'm looking for you now, partner."

Kevin looked the reverend up and down before they both turned and walked away. Then Kevin thought, *I should've punched him in the back of his fuckin' head. What does he mean, ask Stephanie? What does Stephanie know? What is she not telling me?* Kevin was upset and frustrated. On his way home, he called Stephanie to see if he could get some answers. She picked up the phone.

"Hello . . ." Kevin did not waste time. He dove in with the first question.

"What's up with you and the reverend?"

"What!"

"You heard me, Stephanie. What's up with you and the reverend?"

"What do you mean?"

"Look, don't fucking play games with me. I just left the church talking to your boy Johnson. He was acting like he expected me. That bitch also said that you could explain everything."

"He told you that?"

"Naw! Yo' mama told me. Stop playing with me."

"I never wanted to tell you this, Kevin."

"Tell me, tell me what?"

"Remember that night you were supposed to pick me up from the club?"

"No, what night?"

"The night I got raped."

"Yeah, of course I remember that night. What in the hell that gotta do with what I'm asking you?"

"That night at the hospital. I told you I didn't know who raped me . . ."

"No, don't tell me." Kevin closed his eyes momentarily, praying not to hear the inevitable.

"It was Reverend Johnson. He said if I told, no one would believe me. No one would take my word over his. So I had no choice. I just kept it inside and I never told anyone until now. I didn't want anyone to know. I don't expect you to understand, Kevin, but a woman is willing to take some things to the grave."

Trying to digest everything being funneled through the phone was hard for Kevin. The words almost sounded like Spanish and he didn't understand any of it. Moreover, trying to make sense of this madness was impossible. That punk reverend had raped his woman and was misleading his entire flock. He was a preacher at the pulpit and a rapist on the street.

"Kevin are you there . . . Kevin . . . Kevin!"

Kevin tried to gain control of himself, but he just couldn't. His pressure was so high that he could see the veins boiling and moving around in his face. He opened his mouth but nothing came out, and he was so angry that it was nearly impossible for him to breathe.

The car began to accelerate and its speed increased with every word that left Stephanie's mouth. Kevin was no longer driving--he was just along for the ride. The car veered off the road, side-swiping a guard rail. Kevin dropped the phone in an attempt to bring the car back onto the road and yelled out, "Fuck!" just before the car slammed into a light pole.

6

Six

Kevin had to be excavated from the car using the jaws of life. Several motorists slowed down to "oooh" and "aaah" at the car wrapped around the light pole, while others peered into it to see if they recognized the limp body inside. Not to mention the opportunists trying to get to the Jacob & Co. watch that remained remarkably intact--its ice beaming in the sun.

As the firemen rushed to remove Kevin from the wreck, the jaws of life pierced the mangled car like a hot knife cuts through butter. His lifeless body was covered with broken glass and debris, and once the paramedics pulled the car off his lower limbs, they quickly dove in, trying to stabilize him. Then they put Kevin in the ambulance and raced, sirens blaring, to the hospital. Meanwhile, Stephanie was still on the other end of the phone yelling Kevin's name.

"Hello!"

"Hello Kevin . . . Kevin. Who is this, what's happening?" Stephanie exclaimed in a hurried voice.

"Yo, this ain't dude. I don't think you gon' be talkin' to him for a minute." Stephanie paused to listen and started to get slick, because this person was ignorant with a big *I* . . . but she needed to know what happened.

"Ummm . . . basically the Chevy is slow-dancin' with this light pole. Emergency got the jaws of life to get this nigga out the car . . . he all banged up. He musta' been riding out, 'cause I picked up the cell phone a couple feet from the wreck."

"Where they takin' him? Stephanie asked.

"Hold on . . . Where they takin' him?" the guy yelled out.

"If he ain't got no insurance, he's going straight to Jackson," someone in the distance yelled. Everyone in Liberty City knew what time it was: Black man in a box Chevy with get-down in the trunk, wearing Louie pants and a thirty-thousand-dollar watch—a.k.a., street hustler.

"Yeah, slim. He goin' to Jackson."

The guy decided to go ahead and hold on to Kevin's cell phone, since he'd assisted at the accident scene.

. . . . .

By the time Stephanie arrived at the hospital the physician was examining Kevin.

"Doctor, is he going to be okay?" The hospital staff turned and looked at the woman.

"Are you his wife?" Stephanie nodded and the doctor turned his attention back to Kevin.

"He's a very lucky young man, considering he ran into a light pole. He's lucky to be alive, let alone in one piece. We've done everything we can for him and all we can do now is wait. We'll be able to assess his condition better after the first twenty-four hours."

Kevin could hear the voices but he didn't recognize any of them. He tried to speak but nothing came out. Then he tried to move but couldn't. Something was very wrong. *Who am I?* he wondered. He opened his eyes and found himself surrounded by people he didn't recognize.

"Mr. Gray. Mr. Gray, can you hear me?" The doctor leaned over Kevin, waiting for him to respond.

"Baby, can you hear me?" Stephanie grabbed his hand and squeezed it softly.

The doctor shone a light into Kevin's eyes, which were red and full of blood. His pupils dilated from the glare of the light and he again tried to speak, but nothing came out. He began to shift his eyes from side to side, searching his thoughts. W*hat's happening to me?*

Stephanie looked at Kevin with tubes and IV's coming out of his arms. Machines were monitoring his heart rate and paddles were on standby just in case. Her thoughts immediately turned selfish and she began to repeat over and over, "how could you do this to me? How could you do this to me and your son?"

She realized that drug dealers didn't have health plans. "How are you going to pay for this, Kevin?" She squeezed his hand and looked into his bewildered face. Then her emotions did an about-face. She looked at Kevin like a snarling dog and growled, "I hate you for doing this. I hate you for doing this to us." Slowly releasing Kevin's hand, she stood up and wiped the last of the squeezed tears from her face. "Goodbye, Kevin."

As Stephanie picked Ian up and walked out of the room, Kevin's eyes filled with water. He was not sure who the woman was with the little boy, but he did understand what she was saying and apparently doing. And it was definitely fucked up. He hoped to God that she was just a passing acquaintance or a crazy distant cousin, because he would definitely have to deal with her.

Stephanie caught a taxi from the hospital to the

apartment and, instead of waiting for the elevator, ran up the stairs with seventy-five pound Ian on her hip.
She ran down the hall to the apartment, opened the door, and quickly secured it with the dead-bolts and chain-locks. Then Stephanie put Ian down, ran to the bedroom closet, and began digging through Kevin's shoes, throwing the boxes all over the room. Finally, she came to a Payless box that was concealed under all the brand-name items.

It was Kevin's stash. He kept all of his money in that box. She picked it up slowly as if it were a precious baby, wiped the sweat from her forehead, and sat on the bed, placing the box gently on her lap. When she carefully removed the cover, her eyes got as big as a child's on Christmas day.

In the box was thirty-five thousand dollars wrapped in Saran Wrap. There were seven bundles of money, each containing five grand.

"This it? Muthafucka, I know you got more."

Stephanie dove back in the closet, ripping the cover off every shoe box. But that was it. There was no more. She sat down in the rear of the closet with her back against the wall.

"After all this time, you only got thirty-five grand!" She went into her secret spot and retrieved an additional ten thousand, some of which she'd cuffed from Kevin on nights he came home high or drunk, and some she'd gotten from an occasional trick.

After gathering together all of her cash she bellowed out in disgust. She could have made that much in a few months at the strip-club. She knew there was more--there just had to be. But there was no time to dwell on it. Besides, Kevin didn't know who he was, let alone where he lived, so she could come back and search for it later. Or better yet, ask an old friend some new questions.

Stephanie immediately packed all her things--throwing all she could carry into four pieces of Louie luggage--while Ian sat on the floor, looking at his mother with confusion in his eyes.

"Where we goin', Ma?" he asked.

"We're going away for a little while, baby. Go get some of your toys. Whatever you want to take with you."

"Okay, Momma." Ian got up and ran to his room.

Then he shouted, "Momma!" Stephanie replied as she stuffed the money into an oversized purse. "Yes, baby?"

"Are we going to stay with Daddy?"

"Yes, baby, we are going to stay with your father."

Stephanie picked up the phone and dialed a number. She was shaking and biting off her two-inch acrylic nails. The phone rang ten times and she was about to hang up when a man's voice answered, "Hello."

"Come get me."

"Come get you? What do you mean, come get you?" The man sound surprised.

"I'm leaving him for good. Just come get us."

"Okay, but I told you it was over between us."

"Ain't nothin' over. You been fucking me and now you just want it to be over? Come pick us up!" Stephanie yelled into the phone and paced frantically.

"Who you talking to?" Stephanie glanced in the mirror and saw how out of control she was. She quickly lowered her voice, realizing she was in no position to be hostile.

"I'm sorry, baby, I just need you now."

"I told you. It's over between us. I can't have you in my life. You have too many issues. Which Stephanie is this, anyway? Stephanie the stripper, Stephanie the housewife, or Stephanie the ho'. You need to take that act of yours on the road with the circus."

"I'm sorry, baby. I'll change."

"Yeah, I heard that all before."

"What about your son? What about Ian?"

"What about him? Let that other nigga raise him. He thinks that's his boy. Why you calling me anyway? Where is Kevin?"

"Kevin's in the hospital. He was in a wreck. It's over between us."

"That's good for his thug ass." The man laughed.

"You ain't shit. He's messed up real bad. How can you say that?"

"I ain't shit? You trying to leave the nigga and be with me and you saying I ain't shit? Stephanie, please. You pitiful."

"Fuck you! I told you I was gon' get yo' ass. I hope Kevin does get better. 'Cause when he does, he's going to kill you."

Stephanie paused briefly, breathing heavily into the phone. "That's right. I told him you raped me. You think you can treat me like shit and get away with it?"

"You stupid, psycho bitch! You told him what?"

"You heard me!"

"Is yo' weave too tight? Trick, you just fucked yourself." The reverend slammed down the phone.

"Don't you hang up on me," Stephanie repeatedly hollered into the phone and when there was no answer, she slammed it down, shattering it.

"Momma, what's wrong?" Ian asked, returning to the bedroom.

Stephanie sat at the end of the bed, dejected. She had her head in her hands and was squeezing it as hard as she could, digging her fingernails into her scalp and causing it to bleed. Ian pushed her head up and bent down to see her face.

"I'm ready, Momma. I'm ready to go see Daddy. I got some books so I can read him a story."

"Yeah, I'm ready. Let's go see your daddy." Stephanie stood up, held her hands next to her cheeks, and let out a long sigh. The blood on her finger-tips smeared onto her face and she looked like a real animal. And that's exactly what she was: a beast.

Stephanie went over her choices and came to the conclusion that the only one she really had was to pray that Kevin got better. Then she took the money out of her purse and put it back in the closet, arranging all of the boxes so they were back in their original spaces.

"Ian," she called out to her son.

"Yes, Momma."

"Let's go, baby."

7

Seven

All hell was about to break loose. Monica received word that Kevin was in the hospital and made it her business to go and check on the status of her future baby's daddy. She arrived at the hospital in her traditional ghetto style, pulling up to the hospital in her chocolate Impala and blasting her theme song, "The Baddest Bitch." Everyone from the 'hood could tell when she was around.

She stepped out of the car dressed in a skin-tight, hot-pink, catsuit, with a red Coach bag on her arm, two-inch, pearl-colored fingernails, and inch-long acrylic toenails that curved and touched the ground. It was hard to imagine how she was able to stand up because her neck and arms always dripped with gold.

As Monica sashayed down the hospital corridors, everyone turned to look. The loud taps from her high-heels were hard to ignore and the men could not resist looking at her crotch. The gap between her legs was so wide you could see the future. She didn't have on any underwear, so the print of her vagina was very noticeable. Her pubic hair bulged under the cat suit and the hairs appeared to be screaming, as if they were being walled in against their will.

Monica burst into the lobby shouting his name. "Ready," she yelled, as she walked right past the reception desk.

"Ready!" Everyone looked at her. She seemed crazy.

"May I help you?" a nurse asked.

"Yeah, I'm looking for my boo. His name Ready. Where he at?" she said, with one hand on her hip as she popped her lips with each word.

"Ready, is it?" the nurse asked, a bit uncertain about who or what Monica was asking for.

"Yeah, that's what I said."

"The person you're looking for, his name is Ready?"

"Yeah. Kevin, but everyone know him as Ready. I guess that's his nickname."

"Come with me and let's see if we can find the person you're looking for." Monica followed the nurse to the reception desk.

. . . . .

In the meantime, Stephanie had managed to tidy up the apartment and gather her thoughts. She pulled the blinds back to check on the arrival of the taxi. "Ian, let's go, baby. The taxi is here," she said calmly.

Ian had become accustomed to his mother's mood swings. He just thought it was how Mommies behaved. Once he'd heard his Uncle Clyde tell Kevin that Stephanie was a psycho, and though he didn't quite know what "psycho" meant, he agreed with Clyde.

"Let's go, Momma."

Stephanie collected Ian and their belongings and headed downstairs. She opened the back door of the taxi and let Ian crawl in.

"Where to, lady?" The cab driver looked back at Stephanie chewing on a mouthful of tobacco.

"Jackson," she said, closing the door. Stephanie thought about what she might say to Kevin and rehearsed the conversation in her head during the thirty-minute ride, though she was constantly interrupted by the taxi driver's attempt to make idle chatter.

"So who's in the hospital?" the cabby asked.

"Mind yo' business," Stephanie replied in a low, cranky voice, without turning her head away from the window. She just stared out into the abyss--the emptiness she believed her life would become.

She realized that the days ahead were likely to be rough: She'd opened a can of worms with the reverend, not to mention her first encounter with Kevin in the hospital. Hopefully, Kevin wouldn't remember her conversation. But most importantly, Stephanie hoped the reverend would be as soft as she anticipated.

"Thirty-five dollars, lady." The driver parked in front of the hospital. "Yo, lady, thirty-five dollars," he repeated in an attempt to get Stephanie's attention.

"Momma." Ian shook his mother's leg.

"What is it?" Stephanie answered, emerging from her temporary coma.

"Thirty-five dollars, lady." The cab driver paused, looking Stephanie in the eyes.

"Are you gonna be ah'ight?"

"Yeah, I'ma be fine. Let's go, Ian. Keep the change." Stephanie threw forty dollars over the seat and got out of the cab with a Kool-Aid smile.

Perking up immediately, she rubbed her hands through her bonded, waist-length extensions, applied lip-gloss to her full lips, checked her appearance in the cab window, and grabbed Ian by the hand.

"Come on, baby, let's go see Daddy."

Stephanie had the extraordinary ability to turn her emotions on and off. She could bounce from one mood to another as though she were equipped with hydraulics, and it made her more dangerous than Clyde. At least with Clyde you knew where he stood. But you never saw Stephanie coming. She really was a psycho.

Hustling into the hospital, Stephanie went straight past the crowded lobby and around to the reception desk. There she was slowed by the sight of a known face.

"Bitch, whatcha doing here?" A dead silence fell over the lobby of sick and injured patients.

"Hey bitch. You know you hear me. Who you here to see?"

Stephanie walked slowly towards Monica like a lioness moving towards her prey. Her jaws were locked as she spoke between her teeth.

The two had been going head-to-head since their high school years at Northwestern. One of them always tried to get the other's man, so there was bad blood between them long before Kevin came along.

"Bitch, who you here for?"

Monica stood up and placed her right hand in her designer bag as she kicked off her pumps and pulled off her earrings.

"Bitch, who you callin' a bitch?" Monica stood there like she was about to shoot a free throw.

Stephanie released Ian's hand and gestured for him to stay where he was. Then she cautiously moved toward Monica, putting her free hand into her bag. "Bitch, whatcha wanna do?" Stephanie replied. She was in a slight crouch with her left leg in front of her.

"Bitch, it's a whatever!" Monica matched Stephanie's

every move.

"I'ma getcha, bitch!" Stephanie stepped back, pulling her hair back into a pony- tail. "I'ma get yo' ass!"

"Bitch, you ain't gon' do shit, and you know why I'm here, bitch. I'm here to see my baby's daddy." Stephanie's eyes grew wide. "Yeah, don't look surprised," Monica smirked as she rubbed her stomach. "That's right, my baby's D-A-D-D-Y. How you like that?"

"What!" Stephanie yelled out.

"Yeah, bitch, he still fuckin' me," Monica said, grabbing her vagina. "He can't get enough of this sweet pussy."

But before she could finish saying the words Stephanie rushed her. Monica tried to pull out the ice-pick she was concealing in her bag, but Stephanie made contact with her jaw before she could, and followed up with a barrage of blows. Then Monica reached up and grabbed Stephanie by the back of her hair and latched onto her pony-tail like a tick on a dog. They were swinging violently at each other.

The nurse at the reception desk called for security and the two women continued to scrap as Ian watched from a corner of the lobby. Then Stephanie and Monica went to the ground. Stephanie fell on top of Monica and, pressing her knee into her stomach, muttered, "You ain't going to have *this* muthafucka." All the air left Monica and she became completely defenseless. Stephanie pounded away at her stomach with both fists until Ian yelled out, "Mamma!" Then Stephanie stopped, got up, grabbed Ian's hand, and ran out of the hospital.

Security showed up but it was too late. The fight was over, and exposed tits and torn-out weave were all that was left.

Monica managed to roll over on both knees as she

gasped to regain her breath, wiping blood and saliva from her face as she reached for her purse. As soon as security grabbed her by the arm and helped her to her feet, she snatched away, yelling, “Where the fuck was y’all when the ho’ was beatin’ my ass? Get yo’ fucking hands off me!”

Stephanie had long since fled the scene. Monica followed in her Impala with the music blasting and immediately called her big, butch cousin Angie to let her know what had happened.

Angie was straight out of the penitentiary after a seven-year bid for “possession with intent to distribute.” She was small-time and looking to move up when she stepped on the big boy’s toes. They had set her up, and off to the pen she went. As big as any nigga on the street, all Angie did in jail was lift weights and eat pussy. She was *’bout it*!

“Hello.”

“Angie, guess what just happened?” Monica spoke frantically into the phone.

“Girl, what?”

“That bitch Stephanie and two of her girls just jumped me.”

“Ready’s bitch?”

“Yeah, that bitch and two of her homegirls. I was at the hospital tryin’ to see my man and that bitch asked me why I was there. I just tried to ignore the bitch. While I was talking to the nurse, that bitch stole me.”

“She stole you, girl?”

“Hell, yeah. The bitch hit me and her homegirls jumped in.”

“We got to ride on them ho’s. You okay?”

“Yeah, I’m straight.” Monica looked at herself in the rearview mirror. “I shoulda poked that bitch with this ice-pick.”

"You shoulda. I woulda. I would have poked so many holes in the bitch she woulda looked like a screen door."

"I heard that, girl."

"Don't worry about it, cuz. We gon' get that ho', you can bet bread on that. Come on by the crib, I'll be here."

"Ah'ight then, I'm on my way." Monica hung up the phone and drove on with a shitty grin on her face.

8

Eight

Days went by and Kevin slowly regained his strength. He began to remember bits and pieces of his life but the majority of it didn't make sense. His memory seemed to come to him in dreams that were like short clips from a bad horror flick. Every once in a while he'd glance over at the anesthesia his body was absorbing, sure that his hallucinations were the result of the pain-killers.

Stephanie managed to sneak into the hospital under a wig and dark shades to visit him. The sunglasses also masked the black eye she'd suffered during the scuffle with Monica.

She went on as if nothing had happened. "How are you feeling today?" Stephanie asked Kevin as she applied Chapstick to his cracked lips. His eyes were in a dead stare, looking strangely at Stephanie as she stood over him in her disguise. He wasn't sure why she was trying to hide her identity.

"Take your glasses off." Kevin spoke in a strained voice. He talked very little during this time in the hospital because he was leery of his surroundings and the staff.

"Take them off." He raised his hand and tried to

remove them from her face. As his hand slowly came up, Stephanie grabbed it very softly and placed it by his side.

"No, baby, I'd rather leave them on." Kevin looked puzzled by her response.

"Please, I need to see your eyes." Stephanie put the cap back on the *Chapstick* and placed it on the bed. Then she tilted her head, looked down at the floor, and raised her arms up in front of her face. She seemed to be getting ready to pray.

"What's wrong?" Kevin asked.

"Nothing's wrong, baby." Stephanie took off the glasses and looked up very slowly. Kevin squinted his eyes to make sure they were not misleading him.

"What happened to your face?" He struggled to sit up. Stephanie didn't say anything as she placed two pillows behind him. Kevin reached for her and they clutched each other in a passionate embrace. He whispered in her ear as he ran his fingers through her hair.

"Who did this to you?" Stephanie rubbed his back and held him even tighter before she answered his question.

"It was Reverend Johnson." Bits and pieces of Kevin's recollection became clearer. He remembered his conversation with the reverend and he also remembered what Stephanie had told him just before the wreck. He pulled Stephanie close to him and squeezed her with the passion a man has for a woman he loves.

"It's okay, sweetheart, it's okay." Stephanie held Kevin as she smiled--thrilled about the seed she'd just planted.

The moment was interrupted by the doctor entering the room. "Mr. Gray."

"Yes, doc."

"Mr. Gray, you are a very lucky man. All of your test

results came back negative. Aside from a mild concussion and some serious road rash, you're okay. I'm sure you're not a vain man, so you'll be in no hurry to rush your healing. Someone upstairs really likes you. I'll be releasing you tomorrow." The doctor signed a few sheets of paper attached to a clipboard at the foot of the bed, shook Kevin's hand, and walked out of the room. Kevin just stared at Stephanie the entire time, thinking about payback.

• • • • •

The next day the couple made their way out of the hospital. When the nurse wheeled Kevin out, he looked up to see his car in the parking lot.

"I thought I totaled it."

"You did. I bought you the exact same car. Everything in it is exactly the same."

"You got that get-down in the trunk?"

"You know it!"

Kevin stood up and walked towards the car.

"Damn, this shit fly. It looks better than the first."

"It cost enough!" Stephanie had used part of her stash and a lot of Kevin's money to buy him the new car.

"Give me the keys."

"You can't drive. At least not while you're on that dope. You're not about to black out and kill us . . . I don't think so. Not with all them pain killers you on."

"Ah'ight . . . Ah'ight. Damn. You got it!" The two got into the over-dressed Chevy and made their way to the apartment.

"How's my little man?"

"He's doing fine. He can't wait to see his daddy. He made you a cake all by himself."

"He did?"

"Yeah, and it's nasty as hell. But eat some of it, because I don't want his feelings to be hurt."

"Shit, if my little man made it, I'll eat it."

"We have to stop by Anna's and pick him up." Kevin sat up high in the seat, proud and happy that his boy thought enough of him to bake him a cake.

He stared at Stephanie the entire way, marveling at how beautiful she was, and wondered how someone so fine could be completely nuts. He hadn't forgotten what she'd said to him when he arrived at the hospital. Though he didn't remember the whole conversation, he distinctly remembered her saying good-bye. It was one of those "have a nice life" good-byes.

"So you got your hair and nails done for my home-coming?" Kevin remarked.

"You know it!" Stephanie said, squeezing Kevin's thigh.

"They look nice, but then you always look nice." Stephanie didn't even respond.

There was a moment of silence, after which Kevin exclaimed, "Stephanie? Did you hear me?"

"Oh . . . yes. Thank you, boo," Stephanie replied. She'd heard him--she had just slipped into one of her psycho moments. When Kevin mentioned her nails, she began rehashing the feelings she had suppressed in order to put on her show to pick Kevin up at the hospital.

When Stephanie entered the nail shop, everyone looked up and stared as she took a seat.

"Hey, Steph." The girl stopped talking to address Stephanie.

"Hey, girl."

"Where you been? We ain't seen you in weeks. I know you overdue for some fills."

"I know, but Kevin was in a car accident. He hit a

light pole . . . so you know I had to do the wifey thing."

"True . . . true." Glenda the nail tech responded.

It's no secret that everyone's listening when you talk in the nail shop--especially a nail shop in the 'hood where everyone thinks they're the shit. Women listen just to see if they can catch you in a lie, and they usually do.

One of the customers responded, "Ahh, man, that's messed up. I don't know what be on these niggas' minds. My girl Monica's man, Ready, just hit a light pole too. Tore up his Chevy. Damn . . . just like the one you driving," the woman said as she pointed out the window at the car Stephanie had bought Kevin.

Stephanie responded with a cool, "Oh yeah?"

The nail tech quickly told Stephanie that she'd attend to her in about forty-five minutes, so she could sit and chill, or go get something to eat. Glenda knew Stephanie was loose . . . and the last thing Glenda needed was for Stephanie to turn out the shop on Saturday morning.

Stephanie decided to sit and wait the forty-five minutes. Besides, she could get a lot of information just by listening. As she waited, she plotted how she'd get Mr. Ready . . . yep . . . she was going to get his ass, and everyone in the nail shop knew it.

• • • • •

They had a few peaceful days before Stephanie moved on to more pressing issues. Ian was in school, so it was the perfect time to tend to her unfinished business.

"What's this shit about that bitch Monica being fucking pregnant by you?" she asked Kevin.

"I don't know whatchu talking about."

"Don't try that amnesia shit on me. You know exactly what I'm talking about. That bitch came to see you at the hospital. Yeah, the bitch came by. She told me she was having your baby and you just couldn't get enough of her sweet pussy."

"I don't know what you talking about. You better stop trippin'." Kevin ignored her and continued playing his video game.

"You didn't say that you didn't fuck the bitch. I knew you were fuckin' around, all niggas do, but *that* bitch?"

"Stop trippin' and sit yo' ass down somewhere."

"I better stop trippin'? This bitch rolls up in the hospital to visit your half-dead ass. Tells me in front of Ian she's been fuckin' you for years and is knocked up and I better stop trippin'? Muthafucka, I'll kill you." Stephanie turned away from Kevin and walked rapidly towards the kitchen. Kevin tracked her every step.

"Whatcha doin'?"

"Watch, bitch!" Stephanie opened one of the kitchen drawers, pulled out a butcher's knife, and rushed Kevin.

"AHHHHHHHHHHHHH!"

Stephanie held the knife above her head with both hands and her furious face was replaced by a blank stare. The eyes that usually cried a river were red as blood. Stephanie tried to stab Kevin but he grabbed her arm and wrestled the knife from her.

"Have you lost your fucking mind?" He drew his hand back to slap her.

"I ought to bust you in yo' shit." Kevin turned his back and stabbed the knife into the kitchen counter.

Stephanie saw it as an opportunity and rushed Kevin from behind. She jumped on his back and tried to put him in a yoke. Her legs were wrapped around his waist and she bit the side of his head, gnawing at him like a little monkey. Kevin grabbed her by the head, pulling her blood-

and-saliva-smeared face away from him, and backed her into the wall repeatedly until she got tired and loosened her grip. Then he fell to one knee, gasping for air, and unlocked Stephanie's arms from his throat. She kicked and cursed him as he moved away.

"What the fuck is wrong with you? You crazy bitch!" Kevin touched his head, calculating the damage Stephanie had done.

"What did you call me?" Stephanie sat on the floor against the mangled sheetrock wall.

"You heard me! I said what the fuck is wrong with you?"

"Naw, you called me a bitch! I ain't yo' bitch. Your bitch is 'cross town, pregnant with your bastard kid. I'll tell you what, don't go to sleep, muthafucka. You better sleep with one eye open, 'cause if you close both of them, they'll stay shut!"

"Stephanie, you better stop trying me. I let you get away with this bullshit 'cause you upset. But don't get it twisted: I'll beat that ass," Kevin huffed, as they stood face to face. Stephanie raised her right hand and mashed Kevin in the face.

"Whatever, nigga. Go to sleep and see what happens. You don't know who you fucking with."

"Stephanie, don't make me kill you!"

"I'll tell you what, Mr. Ready! The joke's on you, bitch."

"What joke?"

"Lay 'round for it!"

"Whatever!"

Kevin went into the bathroom and turned on the water. He cleaned the scratches and bites Stephanie inflicted, not to mention the wounds from the crash.

"What the fuck is wrong with you?" Kevin asked,

cleaning the wounds. Stephanie walked into the bathroom and took the cloth from Kevin.

"Let me do that for you, baby." She wiped his face very softly, kissing his injuries. Stephanie then wrapped the cloth around her fist and punched Kevin in the throat.

"Get that bitch to clean yo' face, fuck nigga. I got a trick for yo' punk ass."

Stephanie ran into the bedroom and locked the door. Kevin was enraged but knew he was dead-ass wrong. He was going to get some answers.

9

Nine

Kevin pulled up to Monica's place and knocked on the door very softly--like a woman—because he didn't want to scare her before he could get inside. When Monica came to the door, she peeped out and saw him. He gave her a fake smile and she opened the door like it was all good.

"What's this bullshit 'bout you being pregnant?" Kevin looked down at Monica's stomach as he pushed his way into her house.

"Well, I guess yo' bitch musta told you the good news. Yeah, nigga, you 'bout to be a daddy. I knew I was pregnant when you shot that nut up in me. I could feel it," Monica remarked, rubbing her belly. "Break out the cigars, nigga."

"Check this out ho'. You might be knocked up but not by me."

"Ain't you been listening? Remember the car, when we were fucking, the rubber broke. Hello . . ."

"Okay, bitch, you ain't playin' fair. You know damn well that ain't my baby. Bitch, you probably ain't even pregnant." Monica gave him a shitty grin.

"Well, go buy a pregnancy test, muthafucka. I'll piss

on it and then you'll see."

"Yeah, we'll see. That's a good idea." Kevin bolted from the house, jumped into his car, and headed to Walgreens to pick up an EPT. On the way there, he made a phone call to his homeboy, Clyde.

Clyde picked up the phone. He had come to the hospital a few times to check on Kevin but had never come into the room. He had just peeked in to see if he was okay. Clyde couldn't stand to see his homeboy all broke up, not to mention the fact that Kevin was the brains of the operation. Clyde was praying harder than Stephanie for the nigga to pull through.

"Clyde."

"What's up, dawg?"

"You still fuckin' that bitch from Children's & Families?"

"Yeah, you know I am. I keep all them ho's full."

"I hear ya, dawg. Fuck 'em all . . . Clyde, check this out, I need a favor."

"Name it, dawg, and you got it."

"I need you to get your girl to find out who Monica's social worker is."

"That ain't no problem. That's a done deal. What's up with that ho' anyway?"

"This bitch trying to fuck me, dawg. She claiming me as the father of her unborn seed, but I ain't trying to go out like that. I gotta trick for this bitch."

"Awh! That's fucked up! Steph know 'bout this shit?"

"Yeah, my nigga. Monica told her while I was in the hospital. I'm on my way to Walgreens now to buy this bitch a pregnancy test."

"Oh yeah. Big Angie told me them ho's got into it at the hospital. She claim Monica whipped Stephanie's ass, but you know how them ho's be lying." Kevin's mind raced back to the hospital when Stephanie showed up in his room wearing shades and a wig. He wished he was still hooked up to the IV machine, or better yet, six feet under. But he could only deal with one problem at a time, and right now, Monica was the only thing on his mind.

"You don't need no test, dawg. You want me to kick that bitch in the stomach? I'll ride for you, dawg, and that's real. I'll tattoo that ho' for ya."

"Naw, bet that up. I got this shit, but holla at ya girl for me and hit me back."

"No problem, homeboy, I gotcha. It's done."

"Ah'ight, I'll holla."

"Ah'ight, later."

Clyde hung up the phone as Kevin pulled into the Walgreens and sat in the parking lot plotting his next move. He listened to the lyrics of T Double D and realized what he must do.

"I'ma show this ho' how da thug," he yelled out as he switched off the ignition of the car. Then he walked into the Walgreens and looked for the aisle where pregnancy tests were located. He chose three different brands because he wanted to make sure that Monica was pregnant before he moved into phase two, then walked up to the register and put the three tests on the counter.

"Is that it, sir? You know they sell these at Sam's in bulk," the cashier remarked. Kevin was in no mood for jokes so he simply responded, "Yeah, let me get a Dutch." Kevin figured if she was pregnant he was going to get high. He had an ounce of weed he was dying to smoke.

"Is that it?"

"Yeah."

"$43.83."

Kevin gave the guy three, crumpled-up, twenty-dollar bills and walked out. On the way back to Monica's apartment, he drove in silence, thinking he wasn't going out like a sucker. She wasn't going to put that kid on him. The whole neighborhood had probably fucked that trick and he just couldn't see supporting her ghetto hairdo's and three-inch nails. He just didn't see it.

Kevin pulled up to the duplex, and Monica was standing in the doorway, smoking a cancer stick. As he got out of the car with the bag in his hand, Kevin shook his head.

"Why you shakin' yo' head?" Monica asked, blowing out the smoke.

"You supposed to be pregnant, right?"

"Yeah!"

"Then what the fuck you smoking for?" He snatched the cigarette from Monica's ruby-red lips.

"Oh . . . you gon' be one of those caring daddies?" Monica jokingly replied.

"You stupid!" Kevin gave her his mad-dog face, showing all of his teeth like a snarling dog.

"What's in the bag?" Monica asked.

"Pregnancy test! You pissin' on these muthafuckas and prove to me you pregnant."

"No problem!" Monica jerked the bag out of Kevin's hands and took off in the direction of the bathroom, walking a little faster with each step as she looked in the bag. She reached the bathroom and slammed the door.

"Hurry up!" Kevin yelled just before the door closed.

Inside the bathroom Monica sat on the toilet and looked at the test. Kevin paced outside, awaiting the results, and then hammered on the door.

"Hurry up!" He pressed his ear against the door. "I said, hurry up! I don't hear no piss hittin' the toilet. Whatcha doin'?"

"Give me a minute! Stop stressing me!" Monica

turned on the water in the sink. Kevin's ear was still against the door when he spoke.

"Bitch, don't play with me. I know that's the sink." He pushed the door in.

"What are you doing? Why ain't yo' drawers down?"

"Just give me a minute. I'm reading the directions on the box."

"How you reading the directions and the shit in the bag? You 'bout them games, ho'." Kevin picked Monica up off the toilet and brought her to her feet.

"Take them shorts off." He reached for her belt but Monica knocked his hands away.

"Whatcha doin'?" She grabbed her shorts and belt, holding onto them like a vise.

"Take yo' fuckin' clothes off!" Kevin grabbed Monica and she twirled around, with her back pressing against his chest.

"Stop! Stop! Let me go!" Monica screamed, clawing at Kevin's hands, which were attached to her waist. "Stop, muthafucka, stop!"

"Shut up, bitch!" Kevin snatched at her clothing and the seams on the booty shorts began to give way.

"Come up out this shit, ho'!"

"Nigga, you hurting me. Stop!" Kevin tore her shorts and panties off.

"Now get to pissin'." He pushed her down on the seat and ripped the pregnancy test from the package.

"I ain't pissin' on shit! I'ma let you sweat this shit. I'm not doin' a muthafuckin' thing! I can't believe yo' stupid ass fucked up my outfit like that."

Kevin's eyes turned red. "If you don't piss on this stick, I'ma fuck you up, fuck yo' place up. Everythang."

Monica began to laugh hysterically. "Nigga, you sound like a bitch! You snatched off my clothes and now you gonna kick my ass? Bitch, you ain't gon' do shit."

Kevin stepped over Monica and made odd movements with his tongue. Then he removed a razor blade from his mouth like a magic trick and placed it between his fingers.

"Piss, bitch!" Monica, realizing how serious Kevin was, began to piss uncontrollably. She was so afraid that she pissed and shit on the strip. Kevin yelled but it was too late, because Monica had urinated and then some.

"Fuck that! You gon' do that shit again."

"I don't have any left," Monica pleaded with Kevin.

"I oughta slice yo' ass up, you pussy-ass ho'." Kevin hesitated, looking at Monica. "Bitch, I'll be back." Kevin put the razor back in his mouth and walked to the front door.

Then Kevin jumped in his car and rehashed what had just happened. He figured Monica couldn't be pregnant, because if she were, she'd be more than happy to prove it. He couldn't make sense of why this shit was happening but he knew it was fucked up.

When Kevin drove off Monica pulled out one of the pregnancy tests she'd concealed and went back into the bathroom. She sat on the toilet, urinated on the stick, closed her eyes, and prayed. Then she opened her eyes and looked down at the stick. She was pregnant, but it really wasn't news, because her cycle had not appeared for the past three months.

A few months earlier, Monica had gotten caught shoplifting by a mall security guard. She couldn't go to jail because she was facing the "three strikes and you're out" rule. So she made a deal, agreeing to fuck the man if he would let her go. He quickly consented and fucked her right there in the holding room, bending her over and getting to it. She asked him not to cum in her as he plunged himself roughly in and out, but he came in her anyway.

She felt like she was being raped, but freedom had a price, and the price was pussy. She was more than willing to pay. Afterward, she tried to leave but the security guard refused to let her go until the end of his shift. He fucked her four more times during those twelve hours and each time became more brutal. Finally, he let her out by the back door, but only after he'd taken her picture and banned her from the mall.

Monica knew it was his child. The fifty-year-old, red-neck was the father of her unborn child.

10

Ten

It was seven o'clock Monday morning and the phone rang.

"Yo money. What's up, cuz?" Clyde sounded like he was gasping for air.

"What's up, homey? What's the deal?" Kevin wiped the cold from his eyes.

"Ain't shit, just smokin' a fat one." Clyde exhaled, blowing the smoke into the phone. He stayed high--loved herbs more than food.

"I hear that."

"Yo G, I got that info."

"Run it." Kevin was thrilled and sat up in bed, anticipating the news.

"Go down to the Caleb Center, up to the fifth floor, and ask for Ursula. She's Monica's social worker--a short, brown-skin chick with big lips—and she know you're coming. I already talked to her."

"Everything straight?" Kevin felt a bit uncertain as he sat on the edge of the bed.

"Yeah, this ya boy. I hooked the shit up. Relax, my nigga. Just go down there and handle yo' shit. Yo, if that shit don't work out I'll kidnap the ho' and put her ass in a storage I got in Hialeah. You won't never have to worry 'bout that slut again. Just say the word, my nigga."

Kevin knew he just had to say the word and Clyde would execute his command precisely, but Kevin was going to handle this one.

"Bet that."

"Ain't shit, holla back." Clyde hung up the phone.

Kevin pressed the talk button on the portable phone, ending the call, and sat on the end of the bed, thinking of all the shit he wanted to tell the caseworker. There was so much that he was sure to forget something, so he grabbed a pen and pad and began to make notes. He wrote continuously for fifteen minutes.

Awakened by the scratching sounds of the pen on the paper, Stephanie rolled over in the bed.

"Whatcha writing?"

"You a love letter. Go back to 'sleep."

Kevin stood up and looked down at the notes, reviewing them carefully. A soft, seductive voice broke his concentration. "Let me read it." Stephanie was wide awake and sitting up in the bed.

"I'm not finished with it. Wait 'til I'm done." Kevin walked over to the closet and pulled out his Dicky jumper. He ripped the notes from the pad, placing them in his pocket. Then he put on the suit and his boots and went into the bathroom, washed his face, and brushed his teeth.

"Where you going?"

"It's a surprise. I'll be back shortly. I want this to be a special day for us." Stephanie walked into the bathroom. Kevin was standing over the toilet, taking a piss.

"Do you want me to hold that for ya? The doctor told you not to do any heavy lifting."

"Yeah, baby, come hold it for me." Stephanie

grabbed his penis and carefully aimed it over the seat. "Shake it off for me, baby. Not too rough, do it slow and easy." Stephanie shook it slowly and deliberately as the few remaining drops of urine fell into the toilet.

"Wipe the head?" she asked.

"Fa' sho'!" Stephanie grabbed some tissue and gently wiped the head of his penis.

"Is that clean enough for you, baby?" She gently stroked him back and forth.

"Clean it up for me." Stephanie sat down on the toilet and put Kevin's penis in her mouth. He made a sizzling sound as she slobbed him down. Then she stopped momentarily to ask him a question.

"Do you want me to make you cum?"

"Yeah, baby, make me cum."

"No, when you get back." Stephanie got up and walked out of the bathroom, leaving Kevin there with a hard-on.

"Ahhh! That's fucked up, but I'll getcha' back." Kevin struggled to put his erect penis back through the hole in his boxers and zipped up his jumper as he walked back into the bedroom.

"I'll be back in a few."

"I'll be here."

Kevin kissed Stephanie on the cheek and collected his keys and I.D. before finally leaving the apartment. On the way downstairs he second-guessed the choice he was about to make, but quickly moved away from the soft thoughts of compassion. He knew Monica was trying to fuck him so it would only be polite to return the favor.

On his way from Miami Lakes to the City, Kevin stopped at Jumbo's Diner to grab a quick bite to eat. Nine o'clock was quickly approaching so he scarfed down the food and headed out.

"What's up, playa?" an unfamiliar voice called out. Kevin turned his head slowly as he moved his hand toward his waist.

"What's up?"

"You back in power?" It was one of Kevin's faithful customers. Kevin hadn't been on the street since the accident.

"You know it, baby. Let everybody know." Kevin slipped the man a fifty-dollar bill as they slapped hands. The ultimate businessman, Kevin knew his customer base depended upon word of mouth and faithful clients. That fifty would probably make him fifteen thousand.

"Ah'ight, buddy."

"Holla at cha, dawg."

Kevin walked past the man, adjusted his waistband, and checked his watch, quickening his pace.

At the Caleb Center, parking was a bitch, because the center houses so many agencies and services: court, Department of Children and Families, DMV, a library, and a host of others.

Kevin was uneasy because the place was crawling with cops, both uniformed and undercover and he never knew if they had a warrant out for him. In the valuable words of his homeboy, Bow-Wizee, "It's a whole lot of snitchin' going on." He was hoping no one had dropped dime on him.

Kevin made his way up to the fifth floor amidst the cops, court workers, welfare recipients, and general population. He stood in line, waiting to speak to the person behind the bullet-proof glass.

"May I help you?"

"Yeah. I need to see Ms. Ursula."

"Ms. Ursula Newborn?"

"Yeah, that's her."

"Do you have an appointment?"

"Yeah. She's expecting me."

"Sign your name on the sheet and she'll be with you momentarily."

Kevin sat in the lobby and looked at all the strange individuals there. Most were single women with several children who had snotty noses and shitty diapers. Thirty minutes passed before a woman appeared from behind the heavy doors and rescued him from the sea of pissy children.

"Kevin Gray." Kevin stood up and walked towards the lady.

"Hello, Kevin. Come in." Kevin followed the lady--passing all the cubicles filled with individuals pleading their case for state assistance some honest, most running game. He was about to end one of the free rides and followed Ursula into the small cubicle.

"Have a seat, Kevin. I spoke with Clyde. Now, what is it you need from me?" Kevin sat up in the seat, leaned to the side, and pulled out his notes.

"I want to tell you about Monica Washington. I believe she's one of your clients. She is defrauding the state. She up in here telling straight lies."

The social worker struck a few keys, looking up the information on Monica.

"Oh really. Go ahead, I'm listening." Kevin looked down at his list.

"Well, first of all I know she receives assistance from the state, but I know she's lying about a lot of stuff."

"Go ahead."

"Well, she got a new chocolate Impala sittin' on twenty-inch rims. She live in a duplex in North Miami Beach. Her kids don't live with her, they live with her grandmomma."

"Oh really. You say she lives in North Miami?"

"Yeah."

Ursula looked at the computer and reviewed the case notes. "I have her living near the Scott Projects."

"Hell no!" Kevin blurted out. "Oh I'm sorry. No, her grandmomma used to live in some shacks near the Scott's."

"What's the address of the residence where she's currently living?" Kevin looked down at his notes and read the address.

"And how long has she lived there?"

"As long as I can remember."

Ursula sat up in her chair and wrote down every word Kevin said. "Go on."

"Did she tell you her babies' daddies were dead?"

"As a matter of fact, she told me that two of her kids' fathers were in jail for life and that her other son was the result of a rape."

"That's bullshit. One of them work on the dock and the other muthafucka work at the airport. That's the only two I know, but she pimpin' both of them for money. They give her money every month for them kids."

"What are their names?"

"Marquis Fletcher--he work on the dock--and Vaughn Smith, he work at the airport."

"Interesting. How do you know so much about her?"

"I used to date her, and when she gets high, she starts singing like a jaybird."

"Well, is there anything else you care to add?"

"No, that's it. So what happens next?"

"First, we must investigate your claims to see if they are valid. If what you've said turns out to be true, Ms. Monica is in a world of trouble. She could be looking at prison."

"Prison, huh?"

"Yeah, prison. Are you sure this is what you want to do?"

"Yeah, I'm sure. Check it out."

Ursula stood up and walked around the desk, extending her hand to Kevin.

"Thanks for coming in. I'll get with Clyde and he'll pass the information to you."

"Thanks, Ursula. If there is anything I can do just let me know."

"Okay, take care."

Kevin let go of her hand and walked out of the cubicle with a big-ass, joker smile on his face. He was proud of the shit he'd started, figuring that if Monica wanted to play dirty he was going to show the bitch how it was done.

He hurried out of the Caleb Center, anxious to get back home, because he'd been gone for almost four hours. Since he'd told Stephanie that he'd written her a love letter he stopped on his way home to buy a few cards and a pad so he could copy the words. Then he stopped at the florist to pick up a dozen roses. Feeling good, he arrived back at the apartment around 12:45 p.m.

"Where have you been?" Stephanie asked, still dressed in her nightgown. She was smoking a square, standing in the middle of the living room.

"Nowhere. Just needed to run a few errands. Handlin' my shit, you know how I do it."

"Why you gotcha hands behind yo' back?" Stephanie inquired, leaning to the side in an attempt to look around Kevin. He pulled out the roses from behind and handed them to Stephanie with a hand-written note strategically placed between the stems. She reached out and took the flowers, then opened the folded stationery and read the message.

"Thanks," She replied dryly. "When did you write this?" She asked, blowing smoke through her nostrils.

"I wrote it this morning, while you were 'sleep. I told you I was writing you a love letter."

"Yeah, you sure did." Stephanie walked over to the coffee table and picked up the legal pad Kevin had written on earlier. She turned the page so he could see the lined portion: She had shaded the entire page with a pencil, which revealed all the notes Kevin had written about Monica. Kevin just stood there looking at the pad, stuck on stupid.

"Why you looking so dumb? That's my love letter from this morning right?" Kevin just stood there.

"It looks just like the letter you gave me." Stephanie took the flowers and threw them across the room. "Why is you going to see a social worker about Monica?"

Kevin remained silent as Stephanie continued. "I'll tell you why. 'Cause you fucked that bitch, got her pregnant, and now you trying to build a case against the bitch before she put your dumb ass on child support. Right or wrong, Kevin?" He was dumbstruck, baffled by the amateurish mistake he'd made.

"I don't know what to say."

"I figured as much. I ain't even mad at yo' dumb ass. You know why? Because the joke's on you."

"What are you talking about?"

"You really want to know?"

"Tell me."

"Ian, your son . . ." Stephanie took a couple of drags from the cigarette.

"Yeah, what about my boy?"

"He ain't yours. You know when I told you the Reverend raped me? He ain't rape me, I've been fucking him long before I met you. Yeah, don't get choked up now. Yeah, I been fucking him for years. He comes right here and fucks me on the same bed you sleep in, with his son in the next room. That's right, he's Ian's real daddy. He kiss better than you, suck better than you, and fuck better than you. The only reason I told you he raped me is he was leaving me and I knew if I told you that, you would do something to him. I don't know how you managed not to get caught after all these years dealing drugs, 'cause you a dumb muthafucka. Like I said, the joke's on you."

Kevin looked at Stephanie. He couldn't believe what he'd heard. It seemed surreal. His body became cold and his jaws tightened.

"What did you say?" Kevin turned his head slightly, putting his index finger behind his ear.

"You heard me!" Stephanie said sarcastically.

"No, I didn't hear you. Say it again." Kevin didn't move; he was transfixed.

"Ian--ain't--yours . . . " Before Stephanie could utter another word Kevin grabbed her throat and had one hand around Stephanie's larynx. He squeezed her so violently that the pressure brought her to her knees and her eyes began to roll back in her head.

"Naw, bitch!" Kevin growled as he loosened his grip. "Don't black out now. We just gettin' started." Kevin kneeled so he was face-to-face with Stephanie.

"Now, you a real woman for sayin' that shit to me. I bet you real proud of yourself," Kevin said as he brought Stephanie's face within three inches of his. He turned her head and whispered softly into her ear. "Say it again." Then he rotated her head back so that her mouth was near his ear.

"Say it again," he challenged as he shook her and tightened his grip around her throat. Stephanie didn't say a word. She knew if she said anything, Kevin would kill her and figured she was living on borrowed time, anyway.

Kevin dragged her into the bathroom by her hair, pushed her down onto the floor, and held her down with his foot. Taking the belt out of her silk robe, he used it to bind her feet and hands. Then he took one of the rags off the vanity and shoved it into her mouth.
He plugged the tub and turned on the water--allowing it to trickle in—and adjusted the temperature, making sure it was neither too hot nor too cold. Then he picked Stephanie up and placed her in the tub, face down. He sat on the toilet and watched her struggle to break free. It would be a slow, agonizing death.

"Bitch, this a done deal. You looking at the reaper."

By now Stephanie was struggling to keep her nose out of the four inches of water, which became more difficult with each passing second. Then Kevin had a moment of compassion, just as Stephanie had given up on life. He removed the razor from his mouth and cut away the straps. Stephanie leaped from the tub but Kevin grabbed her around the throat. She struggled to stay on her feet but fell constantly to the floor.

"I ought to kill yo' ass," Kevin whispered into her ear, "but that'd be too good for ya." He stood Stephanie up without loosening his grip.

"Get yo' bitch ass out my house." Kevin walked Stephanie to the door, slamming her back against the wall as he went.

"I ain't mad at you," he said, cracking a fake smile. Then he leaned down and kissed Stephanie on the cheek, relaxing his grip.

"Get the fuck out!" Kevin stood there with his chin on his chest and his eyes trained on Stephanie. Coughing and gasping for air, she struggled to unlock the door, she tripped and stumbled as she tried to get away from Kevin.

Then she regained her balance and took off in a sprint. Kevin watched her run out of his life. She was dressed the same way he'd met her: half-naked and in lingerie.

Kevin spat as he turned to walk back into the apartment. He slammed the door and walked over to the window, looking out at the hot, Miami skyline. Then he looked down at his car and saw a brick stuck in its shattered windshield. *Bitch*, he thought, as he turned away.

He sat down in the lounger and rested his head on the back of the chair as he clutched Ian's picture and repeated, "You got to be mine. You got to be." He looked at the picture for an hour before he flew off the recliner, yelling, "IAN!"

Kevin grabbed his keys and ran down the stairs to his car. He snatched the brick from the shattered windshield and kicked at the glass from inside the car until he had kicked it out. Then he fired up the car and sped out into the busy street, ducking in and out of traffic and blowing through every light.

Kevin was on a mission: he was going to pick Ian up from school. When he got there he slammed on the brakes, creating a thick cloud of white smoke. He emerged from it like a football player coming out of the tunnel before a game--in full stride. Running up to the main office, he was quickly stopped by school security.

"Say, partna'. Hold up. You got to sign in." The guard's hands were extended, gesturing Kevin to slow down.

"I'm here to pick up my son," Kevin explained as he continued walking, but the guard kept pace with him all the way to the office. Once inside, the secretary greeted Kevin.

"May I help you?"

"Yes, I would like to pick up my son. He's in the first

grade--Mrs. Lane's class. Ian Gray."

"May I have your ID, sir?"

Kevin scrambled to find his ID, reaching through the multiple pockets in the jumper. He finally retrieved it from his back pocket.

"Here you are," he said, handing it to her.

"Just a minute, sir." The secretary went to check if he was authorized to pick up his son.

"Mr. Gray," she called from behind the counter.

"Yeah."

"His mother picked him up thirty minutes ago."

Kevin turned and ran out of the school.

"Mr. Gray, Mr. Gray. Your ID." But Kevin didn't hear anything.

Kevin jumped in his car and navigated to Stephanie's friends' houses, pulling up to Jackie's first.

She was a fake-ass diva who used to be fine back in the day but now looked like a sack of shit. You couldn't tell her that, though. She would just think you were a hater. Another one who had lived off the state, she had fucked that up because she hadn't taken care of her kids. When the state came in and snatched them, everyone said that had been her plan from the get-go. Now she lived off the money she got from a slip-and-fall.

Kevin walked up to the door, rang the bell, and knocked three times.

"Who is it?" a woman's voice asked.

"It's Kevin. Open the door." She opened and there stood Jackie in a see-through nightgown. Everything on her body sagged--her face, breast, stomach--even her coochie. Kevin covered his mouth to keep from puking.

"You seen Stephanie?"

"No, and don't come by here knocking and ranging my bell all hard and shit. I thought you was the police."

"You seen Stephanie?"

"Nigga, I said no. Why you asking me if I seen your bitch? What, she lost or somethin'?"

"Bitch, you lying. Move yo' fat ass out the way." Kevin pushed his way past Jackie and walked in and out of every room in the house, opening closets and looking under beds. He even got a chair and opened the attic to see if Stephanie was hiding up there.

"You clowning!" Jackie remarked as she smoked a Black & Mild. "Nigga, you off the chain. I won't tell you how silly you look."

"Fuck you. If you see her, tell her I'm looking for her," Kevin remarked with half-closed eyes.

"Yeah, whatever! I'll tell her." Jackie closed the door behind Kevin. Kevin made several other stops at homes Stephanie frequented but no one offered either resistance or assistance. After several wasted hours, Kevin finally realized where he could get all the answers. But first he made a call.

"Hello."

"Clyde!"

"What's up, my nigga!"

"I'm 'bout to handle my biz."

"What, you want me to kidnap Monica?"

"Just meet me at the church on 22nd Avenue in forty-five minutes."

"Let's do this."

"Bet." Kevin told Clyde about everything that went down. Clyde knew Kevin better than he knew himself.

II

Eleven

It was Monday night. A harvest moon illuminated the sky and city streets and it was unusually cool in Miami. A light mist also hung over the city. Singing and clapping cut through the eerie scene because Reverend Johnson always had revival on Monday for the souls that had missed church on Sunday.

Kevin pulled into the rear of St. Joseph Baptist's parking lot among all the other vehicles and climbed into the back seat of his car, concealing himself behind its dark-tinted windows. Nearly forty-five minutes passed before the evening churchgoers began to emerge. Kevin's mouth began to salivate because he knew his time for reckoning was near. He remained crouched behind the seat, peaking out every few minutes to check the status of the exodus. The reverend was shaking the hands of the parishioners as they left the church and then all of the cars seemed to leave at once.

"Wicked bastard," Kevin mumbled as he watched the rev patting kids on the heads and kissing babies. There were fifty, then thirty, then twenty, and finally only two cars remained--his and the reverend's.

Kevin's eyes widened as he opened his door and crept out, cautiously looking around at his surroundings. Then he walked up to a white Cadillac, with gold trim and white leather seats, and dragged his key down the side of the car, leaving an eight-foot scratch. For a brief moment he felt strange because the car didn't have shit to do with what had transpired, but those thoughts were brief. "*Fuck it*," he thought, and proceeded to flatten all the tires.

Then he heard the crackling of leaves and footsteps approaching. He was crouched down, letting the air out of the tires, and slowly looked out from behind the rear of the car as he reached for his waist.

It was Clyde, dressed in black. The only things visible were his yellow eyes and teeth.

"What they do, fool?" Clyde asked as he bent down beside Kevin.

"Ain't shit, just puttin' in work." Kevin slashed the last of the four tires while Clyde looked on in disgust.

"Damn, cuz. We coulda stole this muthafucka, took it to Hialeah, and let them Oyea's chop it up. We coulda got paid. Why you fuckin' the car up?" Clyde was disgusted. Besides dealing drugs, he and Kevin were involved in a host of other illegal activities--car theft, credit card fraud, home invasions, and just about anything else you could name. In fact, Clyde's favorite pastime was riding up to West Palm Beach and robbing other drug dealers. Who the fuck were they going to tell? It was the perfect crime.

"I'm fucking everything up in this nigga's life!" Kevin exclaimed. Then he momentarily stopped and looked at Clyde talking through his teeth.

"Ah'ight, my nigga. When you finish fuckin' around, let's go handle our biz with buddy."

"True," remarked Kevin.

"Go around the back." Kevin gestured to Clyde,

pointing the way.

"What you gon' do?"

"I'm going through the front door. I got the key!" Kevin raised his shirt, revealing his gun. Clyde smiled, excited at the anticipation of bloodshed, and put his hand on Kevin's shoulder as he looked at him intensely.

"If you gon' do the nigga, don't hesitate!" Clyde said as they gave each other dap.

Then the two walked off in separate directions. Clyde went to the back of the church and Kevin walked through the front.

Kevin put his hand on the brass handle of the door. It was cold. He took a deep breath and held it for a split-second before releasing the air. Then he pulled the handle, went inside, and looked around to see if he was alone.

The church was empty and dimly lit, but a light shone brightly at the rear of the building. Kevin knew it came from the rev's office because he could see the guy's shadow on the painted walls.

He felt uneasy about what he was about to do—not about hurting the minister but about doing it in such a holy place. He wasn't scared, though--not at all. Then he decided that this was not a holy place—it was just a building used in the Lord's name to mislead those seeking guidance. The more he thought, the calmer he became and was more focused and certain of his intentions than ever. The minister was not godly--he was the worst kind of person. *But then,* Kevin thought, *who was he to judge?*

He walked quietly with his back against the wall, staying in the shadows. At the entrance of the office, he peeked in and saw the rev with his back turned, returning books to the shelves. Kevin kneeled down, leaning against the wall. Then he gathered himself together, stood up, and walked into the office.

"Good evening," Kevin said in a low monotone as he entered the room. The rev did not turn to face him; he continued to read and stack the books.

"Good evening, sir, are you in need of counseling?" the minister asked.

"Yes, I need information and I've been made aware that you was the nigga to see."

"I might be that nigga. I thought that was your car out there. It looked like the car I used to fuck Stephanie in. So what can I do for you?" The reverend turned, facing his adversary, and Kevin laughed, moving closer.

"I got to give it to ya, you a cold muthafucka. You might be the coldest I knew."

"You *knew*! I'm right here, live and in living color!"

"Not for long!" Clyde emerged from the shadows.

"Bitch-ass nigga!" The reverend vented as he placed a songbook on his desk. "Too weak to come by yourself?" he asked, looking at Kevin.

"What's up, bitch?" Clyde spit in the direction of the minister.

"You two clown-ass fucks don't know who you fuckin' with!" the pastor yelled at the top of his voice.

"Ain't no use in you getting all loud, nigga. This is a done deal."

The preacher stared at the two men. His eyes were slightly closed and he spoke in a low, but firm, voice.

"Every shepherd must attend his flock and at times fight off the wolves." As he quickly scrabbled for the top drawer of his desk, Kevin leaped over the desk and struck him. The momentum of his jump carried him into the preacher and caused both men to slam into the bookcase. The two were face-to-face, locked together like pit bulls.

"What's up, nigga?" Fists and elbows were flying.

"What's up?" The two men were slamming each

other about the room. The preacher slammed Kevin against the corner of the desk and Kevin yelled out in agony, "AHHHH."

"Yeah, bitch, what's up now?" The reverend repeatedly hit Kevin with a closed fist. But at that point the pastor's lights went out because Clyde came across his head with a pistol butt. Then Clyde stood over the knocked-out man, saying, "Yeah, what's up now, bitch," and extended his hand to Kevin to help him stand up.

"You ah'ight, my nigga?"

"Yeah, I'm straight." Kevin stood up, holding his back.

"Kill this fool so we can bounce." Clyde handed Kevin the gun. "Blast this fool, my nigga. Let's dip!" Clyde stood over the reverend and licked his lips.

"Naw, cuz. That's too good for the nigga." Clyde looked at Kevin. He had been in many situations with him but he had never seen him look so certain.

"So whatcha wanna do?"

"Pick this nigga up and put him on the desk face down. Take off all his clothes. We 'bout to get medieval on this fool."

Clyde slammed the reverend down on the table and pulled out a knife, cutting his clothes off his body. He and Clyde used the shredded garments to bound and gag the man.

"Wake this punk up," Kevin said to Clyde. Clyde took out his dick and pissed in the minister's face.

"Wake up, bitch! It's time to meet yo' maker." The hot piss across the reverend's face woke him up. Unable to speak or move, he struggled in vain. Kevin sat where the preacher could see him--in the reverend's chair.

"You up? 'Cause if not, my man here can piss in

your face again." Kevin moved closer to the preacher, took a piece of the shredded clothing, and wiped the remaining piss from his face.

"I'ma ask you some questions. I want you to answer each of the questions yes or no. If your answer is yes, blink once. If your answer is no, blink twice. Do you understand?" the reverend blinked once.

"Good. I knew you was a smart nigga." Kevin paused before speaking. "Now, do you know where Stephanie is?" The reverend blinked twice.

Kevin sat back in the chair with his hand partly covering his face.

"Listen, the only way you're getting off this table is if I'm satisfied with the answers you give me. Right now I'm not happy. So do you wanna make me happy?" One blink. "Let's start over. Do you know where Stephanie is?" the reverend blinked twice.

"Do you know how to get in contact with her?" Two blinks.

"It appears he don't know shit." Kevin called Clyde over to see if he could get the preacher to comply.

"You ever been fucked, rev?" The preacher's eyes grew wide and he didn't blink at all. His eyes were fixed on Clyde.

"I said have you ever had your shit pushed up?" the reverend blinked twice.

"Well, reverend, today is your unlucky day."

Clyde pulled a broom from behind the door and broke the stick in half. The pastor began to grunt and squeal as he tried to break free. Clyde slapped him on the ass with the wooden stick.

"My boy asked you some questions about this bitch Stephanie. I advise you to come clean 'cause I'ma fuck you with this broom handle no matter what." The reverend began to cry and mumble, pleading with them not to sodomize him.

Kevin stood up, snatched the stick from Clyde, and shoved it up the preacher's rectum. "Loosen yo' ass up, nigga!"

Then Kevin removed the stick and rammed it back inside the minister's ass. The preacher screamed. "So this how you fucked my lady? Blink, muthafucka. You hear me talkin' to you. She always did like it from the back. Did you fuck her hard, reverend, or did you slow-fuck?" Kevin kept ramming the wood in and out of the pastor until the man passed out from the pain.

"Fuck that, cuz. Kill this nigga and let's blaze." Clyde cocked the hammer back on the pistol.

"Naw, we ain't gon' kill 'em. He fucked my lady and now I fucked him. I want him to live with that. At least for a li'l while."

"My nigga, is you crazy? This bitch gon' call them crackers on us."

"No he won't. What he gon' say? He just got fucked by two niggas with a broomstick? Then the whole church will find out. This nigga ain't gon' do shit. He got mo' ta' lose than we do. Untie that nigga and let's bounce."

"You right, my nigga, you right." Clyde cut the straps off the reverend's feet and hands. Then the two men walked out of the office, leaving him unconscious.

"Clyde," Kevin called out to his homeboy.

"What's up?"

"Did you take that stick out his ass?"

"No, I thought you did." They laughed as they left the church in opposite directions.

Kevin watched Clyde disappear into the darkness. Then he doubled back to chat with the reverend.

"Wake up, bitch!" Kevin removed the stick from the

minister's rectum. "Wake up!"

The preacher's eyes opened slowly. "I'ma tell you whatcha gon' do. You stepping down as minister of the church. Don't get all wide-eyed. You're going to step down because you have a bastard child that the church don't know shit about. You fuckin' this stripper bitch on the side. Shit, you fucking the whole flock." Kevin paused and looked at the reverend, thinking of the best way to work his position. "Say bitch, you got three months to make this shit happen. If you don't step off, I'll tell the deacons and the deaconesses about yo' little outside family. Naw, fuck that three-month shit! Bitch, do it in a month. We understand each other, don't we?" The reverend blinked once.

Kevin left the church and returned to the apartment to find the place in total disarray. The leather furniture had been slashed and his clothes were shredded. "Thanks for the money, punk!" had been scrawled on the bathroom mirror in red lipstick. Stephanie had returned to the apartment to retrieve her clothes and Kevin's money.

Kevin ran to the closet where he kept his stash, removed all the shoe boxes, and searched through them frantically. The money he kept in them gone.

Then he began kicking at the sheetrock wall at the back of the closet. As it began to give, it literally began to leak money. Kevin had had an artificial wall constructed at the rear of the closet and inside it was more than a hundred thousand dollars in small bills. Kevin only kept money in shoe boxes in case the cops raided the crib or he was robbed: it would be the money they'd find.

He sat down in the closet with his money all around him, plotting his next move.

• • • • •

With each passing week the reverend found it more difficult to stand in front of the church. He was especially frustrated because of the ultimatum he'd been given. And every Sunday Kevin would show up and sit in the front row, taunting him. The thug side of the reverend just wouldn't allow him to be a bitch.

It was Easter Sunday and the church was packed with the members who attended every week as well as those who only attended once a year. The choir began to sing and the preacher stood up and walked to the podium, raising his hands and lowering them slowly. The choir softened from an angelic thunder to a mystical whisper and the reverend cleared his throat as he prepared to speak. He searched the sea of faces, trying to make a connection with everyone.

"In all thy ways acknowledge him," he said. His words were followed by an onset of "glories" and "amens."

"Church, I want to share something with you this morning." He paused, looking back at the choir, then turned and grabbed the podium with both hands.

"Church, there is something weighing heavy on my conscience. I have prayed and asked God for guidance and He has answered my prayers." Many of the church-goers encouraged the reverend to go on.

"I've come to the conclusion that the Lord has other intentions for my life. I am stepping down as reverend of the St. Joseph Baptist Church."

The church members began questioning each other to see if they had understood. A low and steady chatter circulated. The reverend closed his eyes as he gave thanks for allowing him to be a part of their lives, and when he opened them, tears were pouring from his face.

"Church, I have fornicated, lied, committed adultery, and fathered a child out of wedlock." The preacher paused, allowing the tears to flow. "I stand before you and God and ask for your forgiveness."

He fell to his knees and wept. Many of the church-goers ran to his side. The reverend was a master showman and he believed this to be his finest hour. What he'd admitted to would surely have consequences but it also had advantages: Kevin no longer had the upper hand. The reverend had decided to go out by his own hand if he was going out at all.

The church members managed to get their good reverend on his feet and the head deacon went to the podium and asked everyone to remain calm and seated. He added, "He without sin cast the first stone." The Mother of the church, Mrs. Mary, an eighty-three-year-old widow stood up with a cane and praised the pastor for confessing his sins. He did everything he could to keep from cracking a smile. He knew he was still the H.N.I.C.

Regaining his composure, he stood at the podium, wiped his brow with a silk cloth, and prepared to speak. As silence fell over the church and the congregation hung onto the edge of their seats in anticipation of his next words, the reverend spoke.

"Church, I ask that you forgive me for my ungodly ways. I am a mere man and I, too, am subjected to the evils of this world." Some muffled "amens" were heard. "I know some of you may not have the same faith and trust in me you once had but, family, I promise that I am a changed man. I make this promise to you and our Father."

He fell to the floor and held his hands up towards the sky with tears flowing from his eyes as the choir burst into song. Kevin left the church in disgust.

12

Twelve

Kevin had been out of sight for a while and therefore out of the minds of his many customers. He couldn't afford to stay off the streets any longer because his money was running low and Stephanie had stolen his stash. Besides, he felt strong enough to defend himself and run from the cops if he needed to. So he decided to go back to the streets to sell his product. That way, Kevin could kill two birds with one stone: fatten his pockets and find Stephanie. The streets were always buzzing with information and he wouldn't even need to look for her. Her hiding-place would just come to him because a junkie will tell on his momma for a hit.

Kevin decided to start before night-fall, which was early for him because he liked to work under the cover of darkness. The streets were still the same. Each hustler had his spot and Kevin rolled across the top, checking out the set. As he gazed at his spot he noticed a new face working his corner. This nigga had violated.

Kevin noted to himself to ask Clyde what was up. Clyde practically lived on the streets and hadn't informed him of any new personnel joining their tightly-knit crew.

Everyone knew that corner was Kevin's, so Kevin thought the young boy might be trying to earn a rep by working his spot. Little did the kid know that it was the wrong day and he was fucking with the right nigga.

Kevin drove past, making eye contact with the young man. The boy recognized him and quickly fled, reassuring Kevin of his prowess on the streets.

Kevin parked his car four blocks away from the hole at an old lady's house. He paid her light and water bills--as well as giving her cash--in exchange for the use of her yard from time-to-time. When Kevin pulled into the yard, she was sitting on the porch of the house, fanning herself and sipping a dark-colored drink in a Mason jar.

"Hey, Momma Daisy," Kevin said as he walked up to her. He kneeled down and kissed her on the cheek. Momma Daisy ventured inside so rarely that she might as well have had her bed on the front porch. She didn't even have a television but Liberty City had enough action to entertain her until bedtime.

"Hey baby. How you?"

"I'm fine, Ms. Daisy. You need anythang?"

"Momma don't need nothin', baby. Momma fine." Kevin reached into his pocket and slipped the old lady some money. Then he kissed her on the cheek and stood up.

"I'll see ya later, Momma."

"Okay, baby. Momma see ya later."

Kevin jumped off the porch and walked the four blocks to the hole, encountering many individuals from the 'hood that he hadn't seen in a while. They were happy to see him.

"Ready!" a familiar voice called out. It was the CEO turned baser, Dean Smith.

"You back in power?" Dean asked.

"Yeah, you know it. Whatcha need?"

"I don't have any money but I'll pay you later. Let me get a twenty."

"Haul ass!" Kevin told the baser. Dean walked away and Kevin quickly remembered how the streets talk.

"Yo Dean, check this out." Dean turned around and ran back like a pet eager to please its master.

"What's up?" Dean answered.

"Look here. I'ma give you a li'l something." Dean's eyes lit up as he extended his hand.

"Hold on, muthafucka, don't get all happy and shit." Kevin put his arm around Dean but squinted up his face because Dean smelled like a rotten animal. He removed his arm from the baser.

"Damn!" Kevin sniffed his shirt to see if it had picked up the junkie's smell.

"Look, Dean. I need you to keep yo' eyes and ears open. I'm looking for my bitch Stephanie. Now don't go asking nobody shit. You understand?" Dean nodded his head.

"Just if you hear anythang, let me know." Kevin removed a small piece of crack from his mouth and gave the baser a twenty-rock of cocaine. Dean opened his hand to look at his pay. Then he clutched his fist and strutted off, turning the corner and disappearing into an alley.

Basers are some of the most dependable and resourceful creatures on the planet, so Kevin knew that the seed he'd planted with Dean would grow into a jungle. Soon the floodgates would open and he'd have the information he needed.

Kevin made his way to the hole, nodding and saying, "What's up?" to all the other entrepreneurs on the block.

"What's up, boy. You back?" It was Sam, a small-time thug who sold a little dope on the side for Clyde to supplement his full-time job as a home invasion specialist.

Kevin often fenced the high-end merchandise that Sam stole.

"Yeah, boy. What's up?" The two men clasped hands and greeted each other.

"Yeah, I've been holding your spot down for ya. Clyde told me you went on a vacation. I thought you was locked up."

"Naw, playa, I'm free as a bird. Free like OJ!"

"I hear that!"

"Yo, who was that jit' that was here about ten minutes ago?"

"What jit'? I didn't see nobody. Ain't nobody gon' be in yo' spot. Muthafuckas know what's up. Clyde got this shit on lock."

"Yeah, but who got this shit when Clyde ain't here . . . you?"

"I got it. You see, ain't nobody there. I gotcha, my nigga."

"Sho' ya right! I'll holla at ya."

Kevin walked off, uneasy about everything that had just happened. Some muthafuckin body was lying, he thought as he began to set up shop. *Either Clyde got this nigga, Sam, hustling my spot, or Sam got that jit' slangin'.*

He took the dope he had on him and placed it inside a wall that had a loose brick. Then he put a few more pieces of crack in his mouth, walked out of the alley, and posted up. It was slow during the daylight hours and the cops were riding hard, so it was always a good idea to have on you only what you could swallow or get rid of in a hurry.

Kevin made a few transactions with his loyal customers, who had missed the sight of their familiar dealer. But Kevin was waiting for night-fall to really get his serve on.

The sun went down and the basers came out like

roaches when the lights are off. Kevin hustled right and left. His bomb was nearly gone and it was still early.

He had to dump the money he'd made, which was normally when he'd call Stephanie to make a pick-up. With no other options, Kevin decided to put the money in his stash spot in the brick wall.

He walked down the tight alley, which was barely passable because of all the garbage, old mattresses, and shopping carts. It was a perfect spot for a stash, but there was one problem: it had only one way in and one way out.

Kevin pushed through the garbage and made his way to the wall. He removed the brick and placed the money inside. It was extremely dark and the only light he had was from his cigarette lighter. Just as Kevin turned to leave he stopped dead in his tracks. He heard footsteps on the broken glass and quickly extinguished the flame from the lighter. Then he moved stealthily and waited with his back to the wall.

The footsteps became increasingly louder as the stranger approached. Kevin pulled his gun as he ducked down behind an old box-spring. The stranger was directly in front of Kevin but didn't notice him as he crouched down in the filth. Two more steps and Kevin leaped out of hiding.

"Brace yourself!" Kevin cocked the hammer back on his pistol, placing the cold steel against the stranger's neck.

"Yo! Don't shoot. It's me, Clyde."

"Clyde?" Kevin ignited his lighter and held it up to Clyde's face to verify his identity. "Fool, I almost killed you. What the hell you doing back here anyway?"

"I hid some dope back here last night." Clyde kicked around in the trash.

"You did what?" Kevin was surprised.

"I hid some shit back here. It's all good. It wasn't much--just an ounce of powder."

Kevin could make out Clyde's image as he rambled through the trash and began to think about the shorty he'd seen earlier on his spot. The kid was on his corner, Sam was acting peculiar, and Clyde was looking for an ounce of powder. This shit didn't make any sense.

Kevin squinted as his eyes adjusted to the darkness. He could see Clyde rumbling through the trash and broken glass. And Clyde wasn't looking for anything. He was up to something.

"Yo homey. I'm out," Kevin said to Clyde.

"Yeah, me too. Fuck it. I'll be back for it later."

This shit was really getting bizarre. If the nigga had really lost an ounce of dope, he would be in this muthafucka with floodlights.

The two men made their way out of the alley back to the main street, where Kevin was greeted by someone from his past.

"Remember me, bitch?" It was the drug addict Kevin had kicked to sleep three months earlier and left for dead. The man had an old, rusty .38 Special pointed at Kevin's dome.

"You don't look so tough now. Told ya I was gon' get yo' ass."

"Well stop rappin' and do whatcha gotta do!" Kevin gasped, with his hands out by his sides. "Do whatcha gotta do."

Clyde and Kevin had their weapons in the smalls of their backs and were at an extreme disadvantage. The baser had the drop on them and they knew it.

"Time to die, partna'!" Everything seemed to happen in slow motion. Kevin watched the baser's finger depress the trigger and his eyes went slowly from the hammer to the cylinder. Then he focused on the barrel of the gun.

As he stared death in the face, the questions that

had haunted Kevin during the past few months began to surface. *Was he really evil?* The life he led to preserve his family was going to destroy him. He waited for the bullet to greet him. Kevin flinched when the junkie pulled the trigger.

Click! *Click!* The gun misfired.

Kevin was shocked--even surprised—that he was still alive, and quickly hit the man with a two-piece before pulling out his pistol. But before he could decide whether to end the guy's life or leave him with a lifelong scar, the man fell to the ground. Kevin had a flashback of their first encounter.

"I should have killed your ass in the streets!"

The man looked up and pointed at Clyde.

"He told me . . ."

Boom! *Boom!* Before the man could finish his sentence Clyde put two in his chest. Kevin turned his head to look at Clyde, who had the guy's blood spattered on his face. Without saying a word, the two ran from the scene.

The streets that had been filled with activity were clear and the only thing left was the man's body, which lay there twitching. Kevin told Clyde to get rid of the gun.

"I ain't getting rid of my gun. She my best bitch. The only ho' I can depend on." Clyde grabbed the gun through his shirt and pushed it against his torso. His eyes closed in ecstasy as the cold steel touched his body. Kevin wiped the blood from his face.

"Nigga, you crazy for real."

"I know." The two separated.

. . . . .

Kevin ran as fast as he could--cutting through yards, jumping gates, and ducking through alleys. He stopped momentarily to shed a layer of clothing, then ducked behind a dumpster, checking the streets and listening for sirens. After starting to go back to Mamma Daisy's house and get his car, he decided it was a bad idea. Kevin knew that the ghetto bird had been dispatched to the scene by now and that the cops were on their way. They were sure to pull every vehicle leaving the area. It was too risky to even try to retrieve his car.

Kevin made it out of the hole and onto 62nd Street. As he ran, he ripped off the A-shirt he was wearing and wiped the rest of the baser's blood from his face and neck. Then he threw the shirt into a dumpster that belonged to a veterinarian's office. The dumpster always smelled like rotting animals and he knew the police would rather consider a case closed than face the stench.

Slowing down, he walked past the patrol cars racing to the scene. Then he looked back and saw his exit from this nightmare slowly approaching. It was the Jitney, a small, transit van.

Kevin signaled it to stop, hopped on, paid, his fare, and sat in the only available seat on the bus, directly behind the driver. He let out a sigh of relief as it made its slow journey north to the 183rd Street flea market.

Kevin looked out the window, trying to understand what the fuck had just happened, but he couldn't make sense of it. Suddenly, a strange feeling came over him, like he was the "Highlander" and another immortal was nearby.

Kevin turned his head slowly to see who was in the van, and thought to himself that he was definitely slipping, because he always looked to see who was on public transit with him. Looking into each passenger's eyes, he stared momentarily at every one of the fifteen men, women, and children packed in like sardines. Then his eyes fixed on one individual in particular: Clyde.

Clyde was seated at the rear of the van and the two men stared at each other intently before Clyde looked away. Though the Jitney made frequent stops to drop passengers off and let them on, three things remained constant during the twenty-five-minute trip: the driver, Kevin, and Clyde.

The Jitney arrived at its destination, the 183rd Street flea market. Kevin was the first one off and waited for Clyde. The two men walked slowly across the huge parking lot towards the entrance of the flea market. In a low, stern voice Kevin questioned Clyde.

"What the fuck did you just do?" Clyde responded in an equally low voice, "I saved yo' ass."

"Saved me? I swung on that fool and knocked the gun out of his hand. I didn't need you to save me." Kevin shook his head from side-to-side. "Nigga, you done got us in some shit."

"Stop acting like a bitch, nigga. You should be a li'l mo' grateful."

"I can't believe how you acting. Fool, you just murdered somebody in cold blood."

"Don't get it twisted, nigga. You hit the nigga and knocked him to the ground. You was standing over him with yo' pistol out. Who do you think everybody thinks shot that fool? Me or you?" Clyde said matter-of-factly.

"What you saying, Clyde?"

"Nigga, I said it!"

"Oh, it's like that?"

The two men had reached the entrance of the flea market and it was about 7:00 p.m. They walked in and went in separate directions, stopping and talking to every familiar face they saw in case they needed an alibi in the future. Kevin was a little smarter than Clyde, buying a DVD player for his car and having the salesperson write out a receipt showing that he'd made the purchase an hour earlier.

Kevin didn't like the way Clyde was talking and self-preservation was the only thing that mattered when all was said and done. Kevin wasn't surprised, because Clyde already had two strikes. One more offense and he'd be locked up for life. Clyde would've sold out his grandma to stay out of jail.

It was close to eight o'clock and the flea market began to empty out. Kevin walked over to Sampson's to get a bite to eat. It was a small Jamaican restaurant and Kevin was greeted by the owner.

"What's up, rude boy?"

"Irie," Kevin responded, extending his hand across the counter.

"What are you having?" the man asked in a heavy Jamaican accent.

"Cod-fish and food."

"Drink?"

"Irish Moss."

"That's it?"

"Yeah."

"$15.62."

Kevin gave the man a twenty and sat down at the nearest table with his back to the counter, thinking about the dumb-ass mistake Clyde had made by shooting that fool. His spot was going to be crawling with police cars, beefed-up surveillance, and DT.

"Fuck!" he said in disgust. He remembered the money he left in the alley and it was going to be almost impossible to get it anytime soon.

"You cool?" The man asked from behind the counter.

"Yeah man."

"Food come soon." The door of the restaurant

opened and Kevin looked up to see his old flame, Plethora.

By Kevin's definition, she was a good girl--a registered nurse who had an uncontrollable appetite for thugs. Kevin fit that mode perfectly. She had a ghetto body with plenty of everything—ass, breast, and pussy . . . she had it all. She also had three sisters who seemed to be attached at the hip. They were always together.

"What's up, Kevin?"

"You got it, baby girl." Plethora sat down next to Kevin.

"I've been looking for you."

"Yeah, why? I owe you money?"

"No!" She moved closer to Kevin, grabbed his crotch, and whispered in his ear.

"You owe me a good fuck." Plethora stuck her tongue in Kevin's ear and slowly moved it around in circles.

"What makes you think I owe you some?" Kevin closed his eyes, enjoying the way Plethora was making him feel.

"This rock-hard dick I got in my hand says you owe me." Kevin turned his head to face her. The two sat at the table and swapped spit.

"Girl, you nasty as hell," one of Plethora's sisters remarked. "You don't know where that nigga's mouth been."

Plethora and Kevin continued to kiss, ignoring the gagging sounds the sisters were making. Then Plethora removed her tongue from Kevin's mouth.

"I know where your mouth has been." She kissed the side of his face, whispering in his ear. "It's been in my pussy."

"Get a room," the owner of the restaurant suggested as he placed the food on the table.

"Yeah, get a room," Plethora moaned in agreement.

"You coming with me?" Kevin asked.

"You know it!" Plethora replied.

"Whatcha want, girl?" Plethora's sister asked.

"I'm looking at what I want." She picked up one of the hot dumplings and sucked on it—then nibbled it down to a nub. "Girl, what do you want to eat?" her sister asked, popping her lips and rolling her eyes.

"Yeah, baby, get whatcha want. I gotcha . . . I got all y'all, " Kevin boasted as he pulled out a few crumpled bills. The sisters quickly put their money back in their purses and bras. The largest of the four practically ordered the entire menu and they all began to salivate as the free meal was placed on the table.

"Damn, girl, let the man set up the table," Kevin remarked.

"Who is you?"

"I'm the nigga paying for all this shit!" The women put napkins into their shirts to keep the food from getting on their clothes, while Kevin looked on and shook his head. The four women took up almost the entire table and the five sat there and enjoyed the meal.

"So, am I rolling with you?" Plethora asked as she re-applied her lipstick.

"Yeah, if you getting on the 83."

"You riding the bus now?" The other sisters burst out laughing uncontrollably.

"Hell, naw. Plethora, I thought this nigga was a baller? This buster riding the bus." The women continued to laugh and the way they were talking and carrying on made Kevin laugh too. He realized that all the years of catching public transit, and walking when he needed to, had kept him with a low profile. It also kept jealous niggas from knocking the door down at his apartment.

Home invasions were a dime-a-dozen in Miami and

Kevin did all he could not to become a victim. He knew that most people thought the same way she did: if he's riding the bus he can't be ballin'. So Kevin laughed with the women, but he was laughing at them. And Plethora laughed because she knew what time it was.

"Naw, baby, I can't get on the bus, but my sister can drop us off."

"Drop us off where?"

"At the El Palacio, and they'll come pick us up in the morning."

"They can drop us at my crib--or better yet--take me to get my car and I'll drop you off in the morning." Plethora's eyes widened because she knew Stephanie was his main bitch, and she'd be violating if she went to their crib. Unless . . .

"Your crib? What's up with you and Stephanie?

"I don't see that bitch!"

"Oh, it's like that?"

"Yeah! So what's up?" Kevin asked.

"It's on you, baby."

"Let's ride."

The sisters pretended they weren't listening to the conversation but they were hanging on every word. Kevin pulled out a crumbled twenty and left it for the tip as he looked back at Sampson.

"Respect."

"Respect," Sampson said in response. The five left the restaurant.

Kevin walked behind the four women and had fantasies of fucking all of them at the same time. But he thought better of it because one of his homeboys, Justin, had just gone through some shit.

Everyone piled into the small SUV and headed to Momma Daisy's.

"So where you living?" one sister asked.

"Miami Lakes, but we're going to the city to get my car," Kevin replied.

"Oh, you live there?" Plethora asked.

"Yeah baby."

"So what made you move to Miami Lakes? Next, yo' black ass will probably move to Weston or Plantation, huh?" The sister next to him remarked. "You probably bathing in bleach." They all laughed.

"Don't hate, don't hate," Plethora said, calling off the wolves.

"Oh, I ain't hatin'. My man used to live in Miami Lakes before he got locked up."

"Don't tell nobody else that stupid shit," Plethora said to her sister.

"Turn left here." The truck turned left on 62nd Street. Helicopters and cops were still circling the area.

"I wonder what happened here?" one of the sisters asked.

"Ain't no telling. You know it's dangerous around here." Kevin responded.

"This is cool. We'll walk the rest of the way."

"What time you want us to pick you up, girl?"

"Kevin gon' bring me home. I'll holla at y'all later. I'll call ya."

Plethora closed the door and Kevin looked at the women sitting in the truck as they tried to figure out why all the cops were in the area. He winked at the trio and walked up the block.

When Kevin and Plethora arrived at Momma Daisy's house she was still sitting on the porch watching the show.

"What happened around here, Momma?"

"Somebody got shot, baby."

"Ahh Lawd, that's messed up. You ah'ight?"

"Yeah, Momma fine," Momma Daisy replied, raising her long skirt to reveal the .22 she had strapped to her leg.

"Okay, I'll see ya later." Kevin hit the car alarm, signaling Plethora to get in, and the two made their way to his apartment in Miami Lakes. They walked through the courtyard, passing the pool.

"Have you ever been fucked in a pool?" Kevin grabbed her hand and swung her around.

"Ask me tomorrow." The two smiled at each other and went up to the apartment.

"You want something to drink?"

"Yeah, whatcha got?" Kevin walked over to the cabinet, calling out the names of the liquors. "Let's see, I got Raynal, Vodka, Remy, E&J, and some Naughty Head."

"Damn, Kevin! When you started drinking like that?"

"I got some shit on my mind."

"Give me some of that Naughty Head."

"Ah'ight, baby." Kevin crushed some ice in the blender. Then he mixed the liquor and ice in a glass he had chilling in the freezer.

"Whatcha wanna chase this with?"

"Cranberry juice," Plethora said. "You know I like all my shit red. Just like this pussy."

"True. But I ain't got no cranberry juice, all I got is some strawberry Kool-Aid."

Kevin walked over to the sofa where Plethora was seated and handed her the drink.
"Here you go, baby." Plethora took a sip and coughed, putting her hand over her mouth.

"You don't need to get me drunk to fuck. We fucking tonight."

"I don't wanna get you drunk. I wanna get you loose." Kevin moved towards Plethora, kissing her and forcing her to lie back on the couch. He kissed her face and neck as he grinned on her. Then he moved gently to the side so he could rub her vagina. He felt her lips separate when he pushed gently on her swollen clit.

"I want you," Plethora said as she rolled her hips to Kevin's hand motions. She began to purr slightly as Kevin stroked her pussy. He stopped and stood over her, taking off his clothes, and Plethora quickly stood up, removing hers. The two stood with warm bodies entangled as they kissed.

"Come with me." Kevin walked Plethora down the hall towards the bedroom and made a slow left into the bathroom. "Get in with me." Kevin turned on the water and let it run down his back.

"Kevin." Plethora stepped into the shower, squinting her eyes. "I don't wanna mess up my hair."

"Don't worry. If it gets messed up, I'll get it done."

The two embraced, letting the warm water run across their bodies. Kevin poured bath gel into the palm of his hand and placed it gently against Plethora's vagina.

"Ohhh, baby, that burns! My pussy sensitive." Kevin rubbed the gel inside Plethora and moved slightly so the water could rinse it away.

"Turn around," Kevin said, and Plethora turned around, leaning against the wall. Kevin gently pressed himself against her and reached around, groping her vagina with both hands. He began to kiss her on the back of the neck, moving his hands from her vagina to her breast.

"Put it in," Plethora said. She reached back, grabbing Kevin to insert him inside her. Kevin pulled away slowly. "Put it in." Kevin turned Plethora around and the two were face-to-face. Kevin bent down, put his arms between her legs, and lifted her up. Plethora slid up the moist bathroom wall and Kevin stood there with her legs wrapped around his head. His entire face was lost inside her pussy.

He poked his tongue in and out of her, stopping momentarily to move it around inside of her as she fucked his face with slow, gyrating motions. Then she stopped moving completely and sank her nails into Kevin's shoulders. Kevin released Plethora from her sexual perch and she fell to her knees and began giving Kevin head. She sucked him slow and hard. Kevin looked down at Plethora as the water washed away her freshly-done hair. She was popping his penis in and out of her mouth.

Kevin leaned against the shower wall and Plethora grabbed his ass with both hands and squeezed. He grabbed her head and guided her movements. Then Plethora pulled away.

"Turn around." Kevin turned around, putting his hands out and pressing against the shower wall. The water spouted out on his face and chest. Plethora grabbed the shower gel and squeezed a lot out in her hand. Then she pressed herself against Kevin, took a handful of soap, and rubbed it in the crack of his ass, licking and kissing his back while she lathered his lower body. She removed her soapy hands from Kevin and turned him, allowing the soap to wash away.

They kissed momentarily before Plethora turned Kevin around again. She was behind him, massaging his back, and kissed him lower and lower. Then she grabbed his ass-cheeks, spread them apart, and stuck her tongue in his ass, licking it slowly in circles. She had him moaning like a bitch and slapped him on the ass every so often to bring him out of the trance.

Kevin turned off the water and the two stepped out of the shower. He picked Plethora up and sat her on the vanity. She opened her legs wide and used two fingers to separate her lips so Kevin could insert himself inside of her.

"Ahhh!" Plethora moaned as he pierced the outer part of her vagina.

"Emmm!" she muttered as he put himself totally inside her. Kevin moved in and out of Plethora as she sucked on his chest.

"Damn, you got some good pussy." Plethora put her fingers in Kevin's mouth and he held both of her ankles while they fucked.

Plethora never looked Kevin in the face. She just watched his dick moving in and out of her while she rubbed her clit. Then she began to gyrate and shake. Kevin quickly followed suit as they began to climax at the same time. Kevin put his tongue in Plethora's mouth as he released himself in her. Then he kissed her slowly, moving himself from side-to-side to make sure she was getting all of him.

Kevin opened his eyes, looked up in the mirror, and saw a demon staring back at him. He blinked several times to be sure he wasn't hallucinating.

"Was it good?" Stephanie asked.

"Yeah, it was good," Kevin replied as he removed himself from Plethora. He reached for a towel to cover his wet, naked body. Plethora jumped off the sink, scrambling to find a towel to cover herself.

"Who is this bitch?" Stephanie asked.

"Don't worry about all that! What's up with John Johnson?"

"Fuck that punk! I heard what you did to him and that was fucked up!"

"I ain't do shit to him. Whatever you heard was a muthafuckin' lie."

"Yeah, whatever. Oh you thought I forgot? Naw, I ain't forgot 'bout you, bitch," Stephanie said, pointing at Plethora. "I'ma fuck you up." She lunged at Plethora, trying to fight her way past Kevin.

"Back up, bitch!" Kevin pushed Stephanie away. "I know you ain't coming up in here tryin' to regulate shit. You ain't got it like that. I've been looking for you and now you walk up in here like it's all good. You got me fucked up!"

"Oh, muthafucka, I got it like that. Just like that." Stephanie reached into her purse.

"Stephanie, don't do anythang stupid." Kevin put his hands up to brace himself for what was about to happen.

"Put your hands down, yo' punk ass. Here's ya keys back, punk." Stephanie threw the keys at Kevin. "I'll deal with you later, bitch." She pointed at Plethora and walked away.

"Hold on." Kevin grabbed Stephanie by the shoulder.

"Get yo' fucking hands off me." Stephanie snatched away from Kevin.

"Bitch, calm down!"

"That's the last time you call me a bitch. I ain't gon' be too many mo' of them bitches you calling me."

"Okay." Kevin took a deep breath, trying to control the rage he had inside.

"Stephanie, where is my son. Where Ian at?"

"Your son? Ian ain't none of yours. He *my* son. Got that? Don't ask about him no mo'! And about that thirty-five grand I took, I earned it, nigga. So don't think you gettin' that shit back."

"Yeah, that's a whole 'nother issue. Right now I just want to know where Ian is and if he's okay."

"Nigga, please. Go back in there and make you a son with that ho' you fuckin'. Or better yet with that other bitch, Monica. She having your baby, right?" Stephanie walked out of the apartment, leaving the door open.

"I'm not gon' let you just walk him out of my life. You can forget about that! You bitch!"

Kevin realized something wasn't right. How did Stephanie know about the reverend? That was twice in the same day. Something definitely wasn't right.

"Plethora," Kevin called out. "Put yo' shit on. Time to go."

13

Thirteen

Meanwhile, the Department of Children and Families paid a visit to Monica's crib. The investigator walked up to the address on file and knocked on the door.

"Who is it?" an old lady asked from behind a torn screen-door.

"DCF," the social worker replied. The old lady walked up to the door with three small children hanging from her limbs.

"May I help you?" The old lady looked and saw the social worker.

"Yes, I hope so." The social worker looked down at her case file. "Is Monica Washington in?" The old lady looked a bit confused.

"Monica not here, baby."

"Okay, what is your name?"

"Lula Williams."

"Does Monica live here?" There was a brief moment of silence before the old lady spoke.

"Huh?" Lula appeared to have difficulty hearing.

"DOES SHE LIVE HERE?" At that point, one of the snotty-nosed children spoke.

"Momma don't live here." Lula cuffed the little boy's mouth to keep him from speaking and he struggled to remove her hand. "I want my daddy to come get me."

"Excuse me." The social worker looked down at the little boy and the old lady gripped him like a vise.

"Do you mind if I come in?" The social worker grabbed the screen-door, opening it slightly.

"Come on in," the old lady replied.

It was extremely hot in the shot-gun house. There were boxed fans in the windows, blowing the air out in a futile attempt to keep the house cool. It was barely big enough for everyone to move around and the social worker could easily see into the back yard from the front door.

She sat down on an old sofa that doubled as a bed for two of the small children and pulled out a file containing Monica's case history.

"So are these your children?" the DCF investigator asked.

"No, these my granddaughter's children."

"And your granddaughter is Monica?"

"Yes, that's right."

"So where is she?" The old lady sat down in an old recliner, letting out a long sigh as she rocked back in the seat.

"I don't know where Monica is. She only come around here once a month to check the mail."

"Oh, is that right?" The investigator wrote down every word.

"She ain't in trouble is she?"

"No, she's not in any trouble." The investigator continued to write down her observations, never looking up at the old lady. Finally, she put her pen down and asked two questions.

"Where does Monica work and do these children live

here?"

"Yeah, these my granddaughter's kids. I'm just helping her out until she gets on her feet," the old woman responded, ignoring the first part of the question.

"How long have the children been living with you?" The old lady hesitated as she looked at the smallest of the children, a two-year-old boy.

"About two years now."

"Do you mind if I walk through the house?"

"No baby, go right ahead."

The social worker walked into the kitchen, which was connected to the living room. It was clean and there was sufficient food in the refrigerator. She walked through the rest of the small shack and found it well-maintained and very clean.

"Okay, Ms. Williams. I' m going to leave now but I'll check back with you real soon. Oh, by the way, do you have a number so I may contact Monica?"

The old lady rolled some bogus number off the top of her head and the social worker immediately pulled out her cell phone and dialed it. The phone picked up instantly.

"The present time is 3:00 p.m." The social worker hung up and thanked Ms. Williams for her time. The old lady waved as she drove off and then rushed back in the house to alert Monica.

"Hello." Monica answered the phone with her music booming in the background.

"Baby!" her grandmother yelled.

"Who this?" Monica yelled over the music, pushing the cell phone hard against her ear.

"Turn the music down." Monica reduced the volume to a low roar.

"What's up?"

"The state social worker investigator lady just left

here asking questions about you." Monica turned the music off, listening intently to her grandmother's every word. "What did you tell them?" Monica's heart began racing, anticipating the response.

"I didn't tell them anything. But Vaughn told the lady you don't live here."

"I'ma beat his ass. Why you let him tell them that?"

"Baby, I tried to keep them kids quiet but he just said it out the blue."

"What else happened?"

"She asked me for your phone number."

"You didn't give it to her, did you?"

"No, I just gave her some numbers off the top of my head."

"Grandma listen, this what we gonna do."

"I'm listening."

"I'ma move in yo' place for a while and you can move in mine. I'll keep the kids until we can get this straightened out. Okay?"

"Okay, baby."

"Ah'ight, don't worry. I'll take care of it. I'ma go up to the Caleb tomorrow. Don't worry."

Monica hung up the cell and cursed out loud. She knew this couldn't be good. No telling how much they already knew. But whatever they thought they knew, she was going to try her best to straighten this shit out. She thought about calling the center to get some info. Maybe it had been just a routine visit. *It's nothing*, she thought to herself.

She drove to her friends' houses to advise them of her situation. Everybody thought of some type of possible scenario. It was like being in jail--suddenly everyone was a lawyer. Monica listened to the DCF stories late into the evening and pondered the possibilities of what was going down. She rehearsed multiple lines and responses and finally drifted off to sleep.

. . . . .

The next morning Monica went to the Caleb Center by cab. She was going to find out exactly what was going on and she didn't want to drive because the social workers were notorious for following people out to the parking lot and writing down their tag numbers.

Monica arrived at the Caleb looking like a totally different woman. The long fashion-nails and wigs were gone. The sky-blue contacts were out and the tight, "get-it, girl" outfit had been replaced with an oversized sweatsuit accented with sneakers that leaned harder than a pimp in a Cadillac. Monica walked up with earlier arrivals, all of whom were looking less-than-average.

She got on the elevator, made her way up to the fifth floor, and pushed past all the others who were there to see their caseworkers.

"May I help you?"

"I'd like to see Ms. Newborn," she said to the receptionist behind the bullet-proof glass.

"Do you have an appointment?"

"No."

"Sign the list and have a seat."

Monica thought she would be able to beat the crowd if she came early but it was only 8:00 a.m. and the lobby was already packed. Her social worker stepped off the elevator as she arrived for work and Monica quickly jumped up to greet her.

"Hi, Ms. Newborn. I need to see you."

"I'm sure you do. Have a seat and I'll be with you in a bit." Monica wanted to go off but she knew she was caught between a rock and a hard place. So she decided the ghetto approach was not in her best interest.

"Okay." She returned to her seat.

The other social workers began arriving and calling their clients. Monica sat patiently and waited her turn. One after the other, everyone else was seen—even people who had arrived after Monica. Three hours later she was still waiting. So she walked up to the glass and knocked hard to get the attention of the receptionist.

"May I help you?"

"You asked me that three hours ago. I told you I needed to see Ms. Newborn. Now she done seen everybody but me. I been out here three hours." The receptionist put her finger up, signaling Monica to hold on for a moment. Monica was 38 hot.

"Bitch . . ." but before she could finish the receptionist replied.

"Ms. Newborn will see you now." She hit the buzzer and Monica walked through the maze of cubicles to Ms. Newborn's.

"Good morning."

"Good morning? It's nearly afternoon," Monica replied with her nostrils flared.

"What can I do for you?" Ms. Newborn leaned back in her chair and looked at her freshly-manicured nails.

"The DCF investigator came by my house yesterday, asking my grandmother a whole bunch of questions about me. I want to know what's up with that." The social worker leaned forward and punched in a few numbers on the keypad, pulling up Monica's file.

"Where were you?" She asked.

"Where was I?

"Yes, where were you?"

"I went to the store to get some milk and diapers for

my baby. My grandmother was just watching the kids for me." The social worker looked up at Monica with this *yeah . . . right* stare on her face.

"According to the case notes, it says your youngest child is two years old."

"Yeah, my baby two and . . . "

"He's still wearing diapers?"

"Naw, he ain't wearin' diapers. I just meant I stepped out for a minute."

"Look, Monica, I'm just going to be real with you. Defrauding the state is a federal crime. You are currently under investigation and there's nothing I can do for you until this matter is resolved."

"Under investigation? For what?"

"Were you listening? Fraud, you are being investigated for fraud." Monica sat back in her chair and put her hand over her mouth in disbelief.

"Why you doing this to me?" Monica tried to play the "feel sorry for me" card. "I don't deserve this. I'm just trying to take care of my kids." She began to squeeze out some tears.

"Why y'all doing this to me?" Monica's eyes began to shift from side-to-side as she searched her thoughts for the right thing to say. Nothing she thought of made sense. She knew she was fucked and there was nothing she could do about it.

"I know you sent them after me, you dirty bitch. When I see you on the street I'ma fuck you up." Monica stood up, wiping the fake tears from her face. The social worker picked up the phone and dialed security.

"Bitch, you can call security now, but it ain't gon' be no security around outside."

Monica walked swiftly past the security guard and into the elevator. Ms. Newborn immediately called up Clyde.

"What's up?" Clyde answered the phone.

"That psycho bitch, Monica, just left from up here," she whispered.

"Who?"

"The girl you sent your homeboy up here to talk to me about. She wanted to know why she was being investigated."

"And?"

"She told me she's going to kick my ass when she sees me. Clyde, I don't mind helping you out but I'm not about to get in no shit for you or your friends."

"It's all good, baby girl. Don't sweat that bitch. I'll take care of it. So them people fuckin' with her, huh?"

"Yeah. Her ass is about to go to jail."

"For real."

"Yeah, I just don't want no shit out this ho'. 'Cause if I got to, I'll tell the bitch what really happened."

"I just might have you do that. I'll holla' at ya later."

"What?" The social worker held the phone, looking into the dead receiver.

Out on the street Monica paced back and forth frantically. She knew the investigators didn't just come to your house for no reason. Someone had to tip them off. She walked back and forth as she called out names. Then she stopped and snapped her fingers.

"It's that bitch, Stephanie." The people around her stared. She blurted out more obscenities than before and pulled out her cell to call her cousin, Angie.

"Hello."

"Yeah, this me, girl."

"What up, boo?"

"This bitch, Stephanie, fuckin' with my cheese. That ho' done sent the DCF investigator to grandma's house."

"For real!"

"Girl, she done fucked up all my shit. I know it was her. It can't be nobody else. Oh girl, I'm so pissed. I wanna kill that bitch."

"You was 'posed to get that ho' from the last time. If you woulda dealt with that bitch from the get-go, none of this shit woulda happened."

"I know. I'm so fucking mad I could cry. I'm up here at the Caleb--and that bitch, Ursula Newborn, my case-worker--talking about it's out of her hands, that she can't do nothing."

"She ain't gotta do nothing, girl, you do it. What's up?" There was a brief silence.

"What's up? I'ma fuck that bitch Stephanie, and this bitch-ass caseworker, Ursula. Watch . . . watch."

"Which, Stephanie?"

"The same ho' I had the fight with at the hospital."

"Oh, that scandalous bitch. I can't stand that ho' no way. You know she posted up over Clyde house."

"What! Kevin homeboy, Clyde?"

"Yeah girl. He been fuckin' that bitch for the longest and he be smiling right in Kevin face like it's all good. We can go over there right now and snatch the bitch out the crib."

"Kevin know about this?"

"Shit, I doubt it. . . I don't think so. Why?"

"'Cause. I know how I'ma work this shit. That bitch gon' get hers. I know she called DCF. If she scandalous enough to fuck two best friends, she did it. I know she did." Monica shook her head up and down. "I'ma holla' back at you."

"Ah'ight, cuz, call me if you need me. We can ride on the bitch whenever you ready."

"True." Monica hung up the phone and dialed another number.

14

Fourteen

Monica moved off to a quiet area of the building, waiting for the phone to be answered.

"Yeah."

"Kevin, what's up, baby?"

"What's up, baby? Bitch, you got some nerve calling my cell. I told you to lose my number."

"Listen, I didn't call to argue." Monica spoke softly and confidently. "I didn't call to talk about your child I'm carrying, either."

"Then whatcha called for?"

"Can I ask you something?"

"You asking my permission to ask me something. What's wrong with you? You drunk?"

"Naw, naw, nothing like that. It's 'bout ya boy . . . Clyde."

"What about him? That's my nigga. What's up?"

"You know he fucking Stephanie, right? He's been fucking her ever since y'all been together. As a matter of fact, she over there right now." Kevin laughed as he listened to Monica's bullshit.

"That's the best thing you could come up with?

Clyde and Stephanie, that's a fuckin' joke!"

"Naw, the joke's on you, Jack. If you don't believe me check it out. I'll holla'!" Monica hung up the phone and sashayed off, proud of the work she'd just put in.

Kevin didn't want to entertain the idea that this shit might even remotely be true. But Clyde had been acting funny and whenever he and Stephanie were around each other, they rarely spoke. It was almost as if they were trying not to like each other. Kevin thought they couldn't stand each other but there was actually no reason for either of them to feel that way. He searched his thoughts and couldn't remember them saying more than two words the entire time they had been friends.

Kevin called Clyde to see what was up. The bomb Monica had dropped was about to explode.

"Hello."

"What's up, pimpin'?"

"Ain't shit, my nigga."

"Whatcha doin'?"

"Just chillin'."

"Yeah, I'm right around the corner and about to pass through." The phone went dead. It sounded like the connection had been lost.

"Yo . . . hello!" Kevin yelled into the phone.

"Yeah. I'm here, playboy, but I'm on my way out. As a matter of fact, I'm walkin' out the door as we speak."

"Oh yeah? I thought you was chillin'."

"Yeah, I am. I just got to make this run. I need to let them niggas see my face on the street so none of them pie-ass punks snitch. You know how it is."

"Yeah I know. You ah'ight? You sound funny. You straight?"

"Yeah I'm cool. Just sweatin' that shit what happened the other week in the hole."

"You sweatin'? I never heard you say that before. Yo . . . I'm about two minutes away from your crib. Hold on so we can rap and come up with a plan."

"Naw, I'm straight. I'm about to clear it. I'll holla' at ya later."

Clyde hung up before Kevin could get another word in. But Kevin was never on his way over to Clyde's. He had sat next to his stereo, turned the music up, and called from his cell.

He'd never considered Stephanie and Clyde. That shit just didn't make sense. Kevin thought he couldn't have been so wrong about Stephanie. First the Reverend, and now Clyde--no telling who else. Stephanie was a straight slut, playing him the entire time. Maybe he was wrong.

Kevin had some investigating of his own to do and he had the most resourceful person in the world at his disposal . . . Smitty the crack head.

Kevin got dressed and went in search of his old partner, Dean Smith, believing he was the best person for the task at hand. Kevin rode through the dope holes, alleys, and other places that Dean was known to frequent but didn't ask anyone if they had seen him because he didn't want his name to come up in a conversation.

Finally, Kevin drove to one other spot he believed Dean might be. He got on the expressway and went downtown to the Brickell area, where Dean used to run an executive office. Kevin had overheard him talking about it once when he was high. It was a long shot but Kevin needed him. So he rode around downtown for hours and finally located Dean near Bayside, pushing a cart and talking to himself.

"Yo Dean!" Kevin called from inside the car as he slowly rolled next to the curb and talked out of the passenger-side window.

"Yo Dean." The baser seemed to be in a trance and was still carrying on a conversation with himself.

"Dean Smith! Smitty!" Dean finally looked around and noticed the car beside him. He bent down to see who'd called his name.

"My good man, Mr. Ready, how are you today?" Dean adjusted his weather-beaten slacks by tightening the shoe-string he used as a belt.

"Dean, I need you to do something for me." The man stopped fiddling with his pants and tuned in to what Kevin was about to say.

"Dean are you listening'" Kevin asked because of the bizarre, blank gaze on the man's face.

"Yes, go right ahead."

"I need you to watch something for me, or should I say, watch out for someone. Can you do that?"

"Most assuredly. I'm sure I will exceed your expectations. When would be a good time for you?"

"Look man, cut all that proper shit. I need for you to be right here tomorrow around 6:00 p.m. Can you do that?"

"Of course. Now there's the matter of payment."

"You a smooth muthafucka, Smitty." Kevin went into a small pocket he concealed in the door panel and pulled out a twenty-piece of crack.

"I'ma give you this twenty now and a fifty when you complete the job. Can you handle it?" The baser nodded, looking at the dope. "Muthafucka, you get high tonight, but tomorrow at 6:00 p.m. you be yo' ass in place." Kevin gave the crack to Smitty.

"I'll be here and on time." Smitty disappeared into the darkness and Kevin drove off, assured that the first part of his plan was set. Then he called Clyde.

"Hello."

"Yo homey. Whatcha doin' tomorrow around 8:00?"

"Nothing, my nigga, what's up?"

"I need you to ride with me to pick something up."

"Okay, no problem."

"I'll pick you up around 8:00." Kevin paused to listen for any hesitation in Clyde's response.

"Ah'ight then, I'll be waiting."

"Ah'ight . . . later."

Everything was set, though Kevin didn't know exactly what he was going to do. But he knew he had to find out if Stephanie was really posted up over Clyde's crib.

So the next day around six Kevin returned to Bayside to pick up Dean. He made a right near the American Airlines Arena and saw that the streets were packed with a bunch of tourists and others going to see a free concert in Bayfront Park.

Kevin drove slowly through the crowded side-streets and finally spotted Dean, who was panhandling every person that walked by.

"Yo Dean," Kevin called from inside the car.

"Yo Smitty! Say, bitch, I know you hear me." Dean threw up a finger, signaling Kevin to wait a minute.

"What!" Kevin yelled out in anger. "I know this baser didn't just tell me to wait." Kevin opened the car door and prepared to get out and whip the shit out of Smitty when he noticed cops standing on the opposite curb. So he closed his door and waited for Dean to beg his last few coins. Then Smitty walked over to the car and jumped in.

"How are you?" Smitty counted the coins he'd suckered out of people. Kevin just looked at him and shook his head.

"What, you had a sign up saying you need money to buy dope?"

"No sir, that doesn't work. I just beg," Kevin interrupted Dean.

"Yeah, yeah. Whatever, muthafucka. Let that window down." Smitty smelled extremely fowl. You could see the dirt on him. "Fuck all that you talking about. This is what I need you to do."

Smitty could sense the seriousness in Kevin's tone. He placed the coins in a bag he had attached to his waist with a string. Then Kevin pulled out a picture of Stephanie and showed it to Dean.

"Do you know who this is?" Dean looked at the photo, nodding.

"This the bitch I'm looking for. Now this is what I want you to do. I'm going to drop you off at the corner where she lives. I want you to stay there all night if you have to. Hide in the bushes--whatever you gotta do--but I want you to call me as soon as you see her come home or leave. Use the pay phone at the corner." Kevin gave Dean a small sheet of paper with his cell number on it and thirty-five cents.

"Don't dial the wrong number! You know what I want you to do, right?"

"Yes, I understand completely." It was close to 7:30 when the two arrived at their destination.

"Ah'ight, get out right here. Watch me, because the house I pull up to is the house I want you to watch. You got it?" Smitty nodded.

"Don't fuck this up, Smitty. I'ma look out for ya. Now call me soon as you see her." Dean nodded again.

Kevin drove away slowly and stopped, in front of Clyde's house, blowing the horn as a signal for Clyde to come out. Clyde came out quickly, locking the door behind him.

"What's up, my nigga?" Clyde said, closing the car door. The two slapped hands, greeting each other in their normal way. "So what's up?" Clyde adjusted the vent so the

AC was blowing on him.

"Ain't shit. I just needed to holla' at you for a minute." Kevin drove off and turned the music down so it could barely be heard.

"So what you need to talk about, my nigga?"

"Yo, I been hearing some pretty foul shit about you lately."

"Yeah?" Clyde responded in a very strange voice.

"Yeah. Some shit I just can't believe. So I'ma just ask you straight up." Kevin pulled into the corner store. The sidewalk out front was packed with people shooting dice and playing cards. "You fuckin' Stephanie?"

"What? I can't believe you asked me some fuck shit like that." The two stared at each other and neither said a word.

"If you were anybody else, I'd punch you in the fuckin' face," Clyde said as he balled up his fist.

"If *you* were anybody else you'd be dead," Kevin answered matter-of-factly.

"I can't believe you trippin' like this."

"Trippin' like what? Just answer the question." Clyde opened the car door and got out. Kevin stepped out too.

"My nigga, you trippin'." Kevin looked at Clyde who was shaking his head and had his eyes slightly closed. Then Kevin's cell phone rung. He looked at the caller ID . . . payphone *305-555-1012*.

"Hello."

"Yeah." It was Smitty.

"She just left."

Kevin looked at Clyde with fire in his eyes and imagined both of them pulling out their guns.

Boom . . . Boom . . . Boom. Each man let off three rounds before ducking behind the car on the opposite side.

"Why you did that?" Kevin peeked out from behind

the car, looking for a shot at Clyde.

"'Cause you wasn't fuckin' her right." Clyde stood up and fired over the top of the car, jumping on the hood and running across the roof as he riddled it with bullets.

"Clyde!" Kevin called out and rolled under the car to the other side. After that, everything went in slow motion. Kevin fired one shot at Clyde as he tried to flee by jumping off the car. The shot hit Clyde in the center of his back and he fell to the ground with blood spewing from his back. Kevin walked up to him and, in an unconscious state, fired two more rounds into his head.

"It'll be a closed casket, bitch."

Kevin jumped in his ride and drove frantically through the streets of Liberty City. He found the nearest canal and drove the car into it--careful to remove the radio, TV, and DVD before he dumped it. He threw the items in a nearby dumpster down the street and broke the steering-wheel column.

Then he walked part of the way home before he stole a bike. He couldn't risk being seen on the bus because it would fuck up his alibi.

When he got home, he reported his car stolen. He explained that he didn't know when it happened; he just went outside and it was gone.

Kevin ran the entire scenario through his head. There was no way for him to get away with it and he felt like his world was falling apart. He didn't know if any of his life was salvageable; he just knew that it was the only life he had to live. He hadn't planned for all this shit to happen, but what was done was done.

So he decided to thug. It was time for him to tie up loose ends. Though he wanted to shoot Clyde, Clyde didn't know what he knew.

"Hello, are you there?" Dean asked.

"Yeah. I was just thinking about something. I'll take care of you later. I'll double what I told you earlier."

"Bet." Kevin hung up the phone.

"What's wrong, my nigga?" Clyde asked. He could see the strain on Kevin's face as Kevin looked at him with blood-shot eyes.

"Nothing, it's all good."

"Now, what about that shit you just asked me?"

"Forget about it, my nigga. I'm trippin'."

Kevin decided that it was not the best time to give Clyde his due. Every dog has his day and Clyde's was approaching.

15

Fifteen

Kevin woke up at about 3:00 a.m. the next morning in a cold sweat. The sheets were soaked and sticking to his body. His breathing was heavy and he had a huge headache.

When he went into the bathroom to splash some cold water on his face, he looked at himself in the mirror and realized that he never took any shit from the people on the street. Very few, if any, had ever even tried him. The people that fucked him over were the people he knew best: Stephanie and Clyde. Clyde was his childhood friend who had been with him through thick-and-thin, and Stephanie was his high school sweetheart, with whom he'd planned to spend eternity. These two had turned out to be his worst fucking nightmare.

Now the pair was laid up across town with his money. And Kevin decided it was time to show them a true thug.

He got dressed and left, emptying an anti-freeze container that was in the trunk of his car and stopping at the first gas station he came to. At that time of night, only curb-side service was available, so Kevin spoke into a mike outside the store.

"Yeah, let me get fifty cents on pump three and the cheapest dish-washing liquid you got."

Kevin filled the container with gasoline, capped it, and drove on. He felt like the big bad wolf. Only he wasn't blowing down any houses; he was going to burn them down.

Still sweating, he was mad as hell and payback was the only thing on his mind. He made certain he didn't go over the speed limit because he wasn't about to let a silly mistake stop him from carrying out his revenge.

Kevin arrived at the neighborhood where Clyde lived. The streets were never quiet in the city: There were always a few street-walkers out looking to get into some shit. That night, Kevin was one of them.

He parked his car a block from Clyde's house, opened the gas container, poured in some dish-washing liquid, and shook it up. The combination was like napalm--almost impossible to put out.

Then Kevin left his car and walked to Clyde's house, checking his pocket to make sure he had a lighter. He was all set and slowed his pace as he reached the strike point.

Clyde had two pit bulls in the yard but they would be no problem for Kevin because they knew and loved him. He approached the house from the rear, whistling softly to attract the dogs without causing them to bark and alert Clyde. The dogs walked over to the gate, wagging their tails as they recognized Kevin's scent. He held his hand out so they could lick it and then hopped over the gate. Kneeling down, he checked to see if there was any movement in the house but everything seemed calm.

Kevin peeked into several of the windows. They were completely covered except for a small crack at the base of one. He looked inside through the tiny opening and saw Ian sleeping on the couch in the living room. There was just enough light from the television for Kevin to make out the boy's little body.

Kevin looked at the little boy he believed to be his son and quickly changed his mind about burning down the house. It had been four months since he'd seen Ian and he stared at him for two minutes.

Then his attention was distracted by the dogs licking his hands and he ducked down, deciding to do something else. He moved along the outside of the house and stopped suddenly because he heard a strange noise. The dogs turned their heads to the side, looking at each other.

The strange noises were created by Stephanie and Clyde fucking. Clyde's bed was next to the window at the back of the house and the sounds were as clear as if they had been outside.

"Ahh, ahh, fuck me baby." The bed was banging against the wall.

"Give it to me!"

"Take this dick, take it!"

Kevin's lip turned up in disgust. He was enraged and went back to the front window, tapping on it softly. Ian had been awakened by the loud noises coming from the bedroom and had his hands over his ears as he lay on the couch.

Kevin tapped on the window once more and Ian removed his hands from his ears. Kevin tapped the glass again but the small boy was frightened and looked like he was going to run to the back of the house. He quickly stopped, however, overpowered by the sounds of passion coming from the room. And when Kevin tapped on the glass again, Ian reluctantly inched over to the window and pulled the curtain back, not sure what to expect.

"Daddy!" Ian yelled out. Kevin quickly put his hand

over his mouth, signaling him to keep quiet, and pointed at the latch securing the window. Ian unlocked it and Kevin slowly raised the glass.

"Daddy! Daddy!"

"Shhhh . . .Yes, Daddy's here." Kevin pulled out his knife and cut the screen. "Step back."

"Come 'ere." Ian reached for Kevin and the two embraced.

"Daddy, I missed you. I don't like it here with Uncle Clyde. He's mean to me. All he does all the time is hurt Mommy. She always in the room yelling for him to stop but he just tell her to take it." Kevin looked at his son and held him close to his body.

"You don't have to worry about staying here. I'ma take you home." Kevin walked over to the fence and put Ian down on the other side. "I need you to stay right here. I'ma play a little joke on Mommy and Uncle Clyde."

Ian nodded his head. Then Kevin tip-toed back to the house, poured gas around the exterior, and went inside through the open window. He managed to crawl around and saturate most of the front with the gasoline-and-detergent mix.

Stopping momentarily by the bedroom, he could see Clyde and Stephanie through the slightly open door. She was holding onto the headboard and pushing hard against the frame, trying to keep Clyde from driving her through the wall. And Clyde was behind her, humping her like the bitch she was.

Kevin started to go in and murder them both, but that would have been an easy way out for them. He wanted Clyde and Stephanie to see and feel the pain he was about to inflict, and he knew both of them were into material things. Neither of them had anything until Kevin entered their lives and if they did survive the forthcoming blaze, they would surely lose all their earthly belongings. That would hurt them more than death itself.

Kevin doused the door with gasoline before he left and then went quickly back out the window. Once outside, he called "911."

"911. What's your emergency?"

"The man who murdered the John Doe on 62nd is standing outside his burning house on 87th and 54th, and the murder weapon is in the residence. Oh yeah, his name is Clyde Rivers."

He hung up and set fire to the house. The flame took off like a gun-shot and in seconds the whole house was ablaze. Kevin jumped the gate, grabbed Ian, and ran from the scene.

"What about Mommy?" Ian asked Kevin.

"She's okay, don't worry. It's just a li'l joke." Kevin looked back from across the street and could see Stephanie and Clyde outside, butt-naked, watching the house go up in flames. Clyde was holding Stephanie to keep her from going back into the inferno to look for Ian. She had managed to escape with only her precious cell phone.

Yeah bitch, suffer, Kevin thought, looking back at the haunting scene.

"You see ya momma?" Kevin asked Ian.

"Yeah, she ain't got no clothes on."

"Yeah, see, ain't that funny? She'll be okay, it's just a li'l joke." They laughed as they walked away in the shadows.

The entire neighborhood was outside by now and the fire trucks were screaming in the distance. Meanwhile, the police pulled up.

"Help me, officer," Clyde yelled, with his dick swinging from side-to-side.

"My little boy is in there," Stephanie said frantically.

The roof began to cave in as the flames took their toll on the wood-frame dwelling. The officers looked at the house and considered it too dangerous to enter.

"Help me, damn it! Why y'all just standing around?"

The fire truck pulled up just as Clyde was about to lose it and the firemen quickly hooked up their hoses and began battling the blaze. Then the officers approached the naked man and asked his identity.

"Are you the owner of the house?"

"Yeah. This my muthafuckin' house," Clyde responded with watery eyes as he watched all of his shit go up in flames.

"What's your name, sir?"

"Clyde Rivers . . . why?" The officers pulled their guns on Clyde.

"Don't move. You're under arrest." One of the cops grabbed Clyde by the wrist and cuffed him. Clyde offered no resistance: He knew what time it was and he was no stranger to the "just-us" system. He knew they couldn't have anything on him. This had to be some bullshit--mistaken identity or a bullshit warrant. He believed he would be out by daybreak.

Clyde had always had dreams of being on the run and shooting it out with bounty hunters. He often watched *America's Most Wanted* and dreamed of being the most sought-after criminal in America--or at least being in the top ten. In his mind it would have been a glorious thing because he believed his peers would recognize him as a true outlaw. But those were just the dreams of a misguided youth who had grown into a man. There was no glory in being in the back of a patrol car, butt-naked and on his way to jail.

"What about my baby? What about my baby?" Stephanie yelled frantically in the street. She fell to her knees, crying uncontrollably.

One of the officers covered her naked body with a blanket. The house was burning from the foundation to the roof and there was no way for the firemen to gain access to the home.

Clyde was in the back of the patrol car on his way to jail and Stephanie lay in the street lost like a golf ball in high weeds.

Kevin loaded Ian into the car and drove off slowly in the opposite direction. He didn't know his next move, but he did expect to hear from Stephanie real soon.

Stephanie felt Clyde was the perfect contingency plan because it wouldn't take any extra effort on her part: she was fucking him anyway. Clyde had often gone to the club to watch her dance and after seeing her naked, he had developed an insatiable thirst for her. He often paid to monopolize her time, leaving just before Kevin picked her up. Stephanie loved using what she had to get what she wanted and sex was all that Clyde was after. His penis didn't let him see anything beyond her open legs and she was able to control him like a puppet. He was just another piece in the crazy puzzle Stephanie called her life.

16

Sixteen

The next morning Kevin woke up with Ian lying on his chest. He missed the time they shared and looked at Ian as he stroked his head.

It was impossible for him to believe that Ian was not his boy. Everyone even said that he looked just like Kevin, though a lot of folks believe if you feed a kid enough, they'll look like you.

Still half-asleep, Kevin eased his way out of the bed and turned on the television—then stumbled into the bathroom. He pissed and brushed his teeth.

It was very quiet in the apartment and the sounds from the television were clear. The morning news was on. Kevin ran his wash rag on end, allowing the hot water to trickle off it slowly. Then he balled the rag up in his palm and squeezed most of the moisture out before he put it against his face.

"A child was killed last night in an inner-city inferno. Ian Gray . . ."

Kevin hurried back to the bedroom as the news was giving specifics on the story and saw a picture of Ian covering half the television screen.

"Inspectors believe a fire was deliberately set inside this small house because witnesses say they saw a man running from the scene. Not only is there an arsonist on the loose; there is also a murderer. This is *Channel 7 News* . . ." Kevin turned off the television.

"Oh shit!" He held his head in his hands and thought about what he'd done. Everyone believed Ian to be dead. Kevin's problems just kept increasing. Now he was not only an arsonist--he was also a kidnapper. There was no easy way for him to undo any of this shit.

. . . . .

Stephanie found herself in unfamiliar territory. With no one in her immediate reach to misuse, she was left to grieve for Ian. Her phone was full of messages from friends wanting to know what happened. Usually, she would have jumped at the opportunity to receive the attention from friends but she was in a daze, going back and forth between being a grieving mother and wondering where would she get her next hand-out.

She had been able to get clothing and temporary shelter from the Red Cross, but for the most part, she was ass out. She had absolutely nothing because everything she owned had gone up in the blaze. The thirty-five thousand she stole from Kevin had burned up too. And her meal ticket and new nigga was in jail, about to catch a murder case.

Believing Ian was dead, Stephanie decided to go by the church to let the reverend know what happened. She caught the bus to St. Joseph's. There was a small gathering of church members outside under a tent: they were having their weekly dinner sale.

Stephanie wove her way through the maze of people. Spotting the reverend, she moved quickly in his direction and stood next to him looking like a sick puppy, while he engaged some of the Mothers in the church. He noticed her and quickly excused himself.

"Excuse me, Sisters," he said to the ladies. They nodded and looked at Stephanie judgmentally.

The reverend spoke with his teeth clenched, smiling the entire time. "What are you doing here?" He grabbed Stephanie by the arm and walked her away from the crowd. "I don't want shit to do with you." The preacher pointed his finger in her face. She held her head down and looked at his shoes as he chastised her.

"Look at me when I'm talking to you." The reverend reached out, grabbed Stephanie under the chin, and raised her head so he could look her in the eye. He was shocked to find those stone, unyielding eyes full of pain and sorrow.

"What's wrong with you?" Stephanie didn't respond--she just stood there. The pastor put one hand on her shoulder and gently wiped a tear from her face with the other. "What's the matter?" Stephanie looked at the reverend with her bottom lip shaking. She opened her mouth but it was difficult for her to speak.

"Ian . . ." She put her hand over her mouth.

"Ian, what's wrong with Ian?"

"Ian is gone."

"Gone where?"

"He's gone. Ian is dead."

"What!" The reverend grabbed Stephanie and held her tight. "I'm so sorry, Stephanie. I'm so sorry, baby." By that time all the other church members saw what was going on and a few came over to offer assistance, though they were really just being nosy.

"Is everything okay, Reverend?" the ladies asked.

"No, Sisters. This woman's child has gone up to the Heavenly Father." The reverend released Stephanie, pulling his trousers up by the waist and pointing his finger towards the sky. "The Lord has called his name and told him to come home." He had to regain self-control because he was about to put on a show, so he cleared his throat. One of the older ladies began questioning Stephanie.

"What happened, baby?"

"He was killed in a fire last night." Stephanie broke down, unable to control herself, and the Sisters took over, moving the reverend out of the way.

"That's right, baby, get it out." They encouraged Stephanie to cry and release her emotions, waving the reverend away. He stood there looking as lost as a bastard child at a family reunion, asking who his daddy was. Reluctantly, the rev walked away from the women, concerned about what Stephanie might say.

"Was that your baby I saw on the news this morning?" Stephanie wiped the snot from her nose.

"I don't know. I didn't see it. It probably was."

"Well bless your heart." The ladies held Stephanie and offered her water and food. Unable to stay away any longer, the reverend walked back to where Stephanie was seated.

"How is everything?" He was very concerned because he didn't know what might have been said during his absence.

"Reverend, this young woman is in need of spiritual

guidance. We believe you need to speak with her." The ladies stood up, rubbing Stephanie's back and reassuring her that everything was going to be okay. Then they walked off, leaving Reverend Johnson and Stephanie alone.

"What happened?"

"I don't know. One minute I was 'sleep, and the next, the house was on fire. I ran through the house trying to find him but the whole thing was burning and full of smoke. I got out and I thought maybe he'd already gotten out. I looked around outside but he was nowhere to be found. My baby burnt up in the house. My baby . . ."

Stephanie burst into tears. The reverend was quiet momentarily and consoled her with the affection a mother has for a hurt child. Then he asked the question that caused Stephanie to turn off the water show and push him away.

"Where was Kevin?"

"He wasn't there." Stephanie wiped her face, looking off in the distance. The reverend could detect the deception. He was sure something had happened to Ian, but he was not certain that Stephanie was telling him the entire story.

"So where is he now?" he asked.

"I don't know where he is. He's probably home. Why?"

"You all were not together when this horrible tragedy occurred?" he fished.

"No, I was staying with a friend."

"Oh, I see now." The reverend nodded his head.

"So when are you going to tell him?"

"Tell him what!"

"About Ian."

"Ian ain't his son," Stephanie said in a loud, huffy

voice. "Ian yo' son. I'm tellin' you."

"Calm down. I just asked." The reverend looked around to see if Stephanie's outburst had attracted attention.

"You don't give a shit about me--you never have. I was just something for you to fuck. I came up here to tell you our son is dead and you don't even shed a tear. You probably fucking happy. I wish I woulda never met your triflin' ass."

Stephanie threw her plate of food on the reverend and stormed off the church grounds. He brushed it off. "Is everything all right?" one of the older ladies asked.

"Yes, Sister, everything is fine." The reverend took a handkerchief and wiped his face.

Stephanie ran from the church, feeling hopeless and alone. One of her purposes for living was gone and taking her own life seemed the ideal way out of the nightmare. She did not know how to pick up the few pieces of her life or where to begin. All of the games she had played were now over and suicide seemed like her only option, but she was too vain for that.

Her thoughts were interrupted by the blowing of a horn. She stopped and looked up at the car. It was a chocolate Impala, with "The Baddest Bitch" blaring from the massive speakers in the trunk. It was Monica, and she stepped out of the car with a posse.

"What's up now, bitch?"

"What's up, bitch?" Stephanie looked at the four women, sizing them up. She knew she couldn't win so she decided to play the sympathy card.

"I don't have time for this now. I just lost my son."

"Bitch, I wouldn't give a fuck if you lost yo' momma.

What I want to know is why you sent them crackers fucking with me?"

"I don't know what you talkin' about." Stephanie looked puzzled.

"Ho', don't try and act like you don't know what this 'bout. You know you called DCF on me. Bitch, look at my stomach." Monica pulled her shirt against her belly, revealing the baby inside her.

"I got a baby on the way and you playing games with my cheese. Bitch, you got me fucked up."

Monica walked up to Stephanie and swung on her but her swing went wild. Stephanie hopped back and threw up her set. The four women circled Stephanie.

Monica's dyke cousin, Angie, connected with the first blow--a mean one to Stephanie's temple. Stephanie immediately fell down and folded up into a fetal position. The women kicked her repeatedly until she bled from the mouth.

"What's up now, bitch?" Monica asked before delivering the final strike to Stephanie's mid-section. Stephanie let out a loud gasp.

"Cut that bitch hair off!" Monica yelled out to her cousin. Angie pulled out a box-cutter, grabbed a handful of Stephanie's hair, and cut it next to her scalp.

"Now what? Keep yo' fuckin' nose out my business," Monica said, bending over Stephanie's immobile body. "Stay away from Kevin too, bitch. He belongs to me."

"Come on, girl. Somebody comin'!" Angie yelled out.

"Let's go!" The crew drove off, leaving Stephanie's battered body in the street.

. . . . .

At the county jail Clyde was cracking under the pressure. The cops told him they had a murder weapon and an eyewitness. His dumb ass believed them, but he had a plan of his own.

"You got the wrong nigga," Clyde explained to the detective.

"No, I don't think so. You killed that man, didn't you?"

"I didn't kill him, but I know who did. I saw the whole thing."

That was exactly why Clyde wasn't the brains of the operation: He implicated himself in an incident that hadn't even been proved. The police grinned at his foolish mistake. They knew they had him—if not for the murder, at least as "accessory after the fact."

"Tell us."

"I ain't tellin' y'all shit until I see a lawyer. I want a deal. I'll tell you everything you need to know, but I don't want to do another day."

"We don't have to deal. We got you."

"Give us a name."

"I ain't giving y'all shit until I see a lawyer. I need a public defender--one of them free muthafuckas."

The cops walked out of the tiny room, leaving Clyde alone. Every asshole had the right to seek counsel, even a fool. Clyde sat back in his chair, confident about what he was going to do. The cops re-entered the room thirty minutes later with a public defender, Mr. White.

"You won't do any time if you give up the shooter."

"We want that on paper," Mr. White said.

"No problem." The detectives left and two other cops

came in to return Clyde to his temporary residence. Clyde wasn't speaking with a public defender--he was talking to a cop.

Clyde was on the sixth floor of the Miami-Dade county jail. It was the exclusive floor for serious offenders and every person up there was looking at fifteen years or better. Some of them were habitual. Twenty-five with an L was their fate.

If Clyde wasn't going out like that, he had to play his hand right. He was going to tell the cops Kevin beat up the baser for revenge and shot him in cold blood.

Clyde lay in bed that night rehearsing what he was going to say. He didn't want to stumble or make any slips because he knew the detectives would grill him repeatedly about the sequence of events. He had to remain consistent, so he lay there moving his lips and repeating the scenario over and over until he had it down.

He repeated it so much that it replaced the truth. But that was the way it had to be: It was Kevin's ass or his, so the choice was easy. The next morning the detectives removed Clyde from his cell.

"We worked a deal with the DA."

"Let's get to it! Let's see the terms."

"In exchange for you giving us the shooter, you walk. That's it in a nutshell."

Without hesitation, Clyde gave the detectives everything they needed. He told them Kevin killed the man and gave them Kevin's name, aliases, address, a description, and everything else he could think of.

"Are you sure this is what happened?" the detectives asked Clyde, looking into his yellow eyes. "Don't fuck us!" They took the information like a dog with a bone and ran with it.

"Relax, it's all good." Clyde said with a reassuring smirk on his face.

17

Seventeen

Kevin talked with Ian about what was happening and told him what he believed would happen next. He knew he couldn't keep Ian locked in the apartment forever. Besides, he didn't want that for his boy.

He convinced Ian that the only way out of the situation was for Ian to lie and say he had run away the night before and called Kevin. Kevin would tell the police that he had tried to contact Ian's mother via her cell phone, but there was no answer and he only realized what had happened after seeing the boy's picture on the news. It all seemed so *Matlock*, but Kevin had no other options. The shit had hit the fan in more ways than he could have ever imagined.

Once Kevin was secure in knowing that Ian had the information down, he drilled the boy one last time on what he was going to say and emphasized that he not mention the fire or the fact that he had been at the house. Ian said he understood and the two went to the police station. Despite Ian's young age, he was very skilled at deception because he had witnessed the best working her talent since birth. Besides, Stephanie had used Ian as an alibi when she needed to prove her whereabouts to Kevin. So this was nothing new for him.

"You all right, little man?"

"Yeah."

"You scared? Don't ever be scared. It's going to be fine, everything is going to be fine." Kevin tried to reassure Ian but he was also reassuring himself.

He pulled up to the sub-station and got out of the car. Ian walked around and grabbed his hand and Kevin took a deep breath before they walked into the station. A chill ran through Kevin's body. His arms were covered with goose-bumps and the palms of his hands were sweating profusely. He walked up to the desk where a female officer was seated behind protective glass.

"May I help you?" Kevin got a lump in his throat and when he opened his mouth, nothing came out. He looked down at Ian.

"Sir, may I help you?" Kevin's focus returned to the lady and words began to flow out of his mouth.

"Yes. My name is Kevin Gray and this is my son, Ian. Last night he ran away from home and somehow managed to make his way over to my house." The officer looked a little puzzled. "His mother and I don't stay together. But anyway, I woke up this morning and saw his face on the news. They said he had been killed in a fire."

The officer looked at Kevin. Then she stood up so she could see over the high counter and looked down at Ian.

"Is he okay?"

"Yes, he's fine. I just want to clear up this matter."

The officer buzzed Kevin in through a four-inch security door and his heart fluttered. He was in the belly of what he believed all his life to be the beast: the police station. The officer made a phone call and Kevin remained poised, awaiting her instructions.

"Okay, sir. Go down this hall and make a right. Detective Passley will assist you." She pointed the way. Kevin thanked her and walked down the hall. He felt like he was taking baby steps because he knew there was no turning back.

"Mr. Gray." Two detectives and a uniformed officer greeted Kevin and waved him into an interrogation room.

"I know someone who is going to love to see you," one of the detectives said to Ian. Everyone at the station was familiar with the story.

"So, Mr. Gray." Their focus turned to Kevin. "This must have been a shock to you."

"Yes it was. I'm just glad Ian is safe. My heart dropped when I saw his school photo on the news. I just couldn't believe it."

The officers looked at Kevin strangely because his words did not match his appearance. Here he was, a young black male with a mouth full of gold teeth, delivering a seemingly intelligent conversation. They switched their attention to Ian.

"Would you like a soda and some cookies, young man?" one of the detectives asked the boy. Ian nodded and the detective asked the uniformed officer to take him to get the treats.

As soon as the door closed and Ian was out of the room the inquisition began.

"So where were you last night? What type of clothes were you wearing yesterday? What time did you see Ian? Did you pick him up? What did he say when you saw him? What was he wearing? Why didn't you call his mother? How do you think he got out of the house? Does this seem fishy to you?"

There was an onslaught of questions but Kevin was

well-prepared and defused all of the concerns the officers had.

"Do you mind if we question your son?" Without a change in facial expression or breathing Kevin told them to go ahead. The detectives left Kevin in the room. Obviously they were going to question Ian. But Kevin was not concerned because he was sure that Ian would stick to the plan they'd laid out. Well, he hoped he would.

Fifteen minutes later the detectives returned. Kevin was smoking a square with his feet propped up on the table.

"Well, Mr. Gray, everything checked out. We are going to try to contact Ian's mother."

"I'm glad this matter is cleared up. I'll try and contact her immediately. I'm sure she must be horrified." Kevin stood up and tried to leave.

"Hold on, Mr. Gray. Ian is with one of the officers and they're attempting contact now. We have some other pressing issues to discuss with you."

Kevin's nostrils flared and he did a mental rewind of everything that had just happened. But nothing had been said that would cause them to detain him.

"What concerns do you have, detective?" Kevin sat back down and extinguished his cigarette.

"Murder!"

"Murder!" Kevin stood up abruptly, causing the chair to rock back and fall violently to the floor.

"Calm down, Mr. Gray," the officer said, with both hands in front of him. "Just settle down." The other officer picked up Kevin's chair and asked him to take a seat. "What can you tell me about the murder of Ulysses Bryant?"

"Who? I don't know a Ulysses Brian, Braggs, whatever you said, and I sure the fuck don't know anything about a murder."

"Well, we have an eyewitness willing to testify that you do. Do you want to tell us about it? But before you do, you're under arrest. You have the right to remain silent . . ."

Kevin looked at the officer as he read him his Miranda rights. He felt like an ass: he'd hand-delivered himself to the lions' den--only he wasn't Daniel. He knew Clyde had flipped the script on him so he just sat there silently.

"Right now you are the prime suspect in a murder case. Quite frankly we got your black ass. So you might as well talk to us." Kevin sat there. He leaned back in the chair.

"Y'all ain't got shit on me. Don't even waste my muthafuckin' time. I want to speak to a lawyer." Kevin put his feet back up on the table. The officer slapped them off.

"The show is over, boy. Turn around and put your hands on that wall." The officers cuffed Kevin and led him away to a cell. He passed Ian in the hallway drinking a soda and eating cookies.

"I said what you told me to say, Daddy. I said what you told me!" Ian said as he burst into tears.

"Don't cry for me! Don't ever let me see a tear come out of your eye. You a man! Cry liquor, but don't ever let me see you cry!" Kevin yelled as the officers ushered him down the hall.

The little boy stood there distraught and alone.

18

Eighteen

Stephanie managed to pick herself up and assess the physical damage she'd endured. She put her hand to her lips but quickly removed it because of the pain, and spat to keep from swallowing the blood coming out of her mouth.

But her heart was in more pain than her body. She knew she wasn't shit and an ass-whipping was in line with her type of lifestyle.

Despite all that had happened she wasn't angry at Monica: it was all part of this ghetto shit. However, Stephanie did believe in an eye-for-an-eye and she was definitely going to get that bitch back.

Sitting on the curb of the street, she began to cry. She could believe all this shit was happening, but not at the same time. What else could possibly go wrong? Then a white Cadillac pulled up. Its window went down slowly. It was the reverend.

"What happened to you?"

"What do it look like?" Stephanie replied. The reverend turned on his hazards and got out of the car. He stood over Stephanie momentarily before taking a seat next to her.

"Wipe off your face. You're bleeding." He handed Stephanie a handkerchief and his lips turned up as he shook his head. "When are you going to give up this foolish lifestyle?" He took the bloody handkerchief from Stephanie and wiped her brow.

"This is all I know. This is what I am." Stephanie winced slightly.

"I know you're hurt about your boy. I mean our boy. But the sun is going to rise tomorrow whether you're ready for it or not."

Stephanie took the nasty handkerchief from the preacher.

"I know that and I don't wanna hear one of your sermons right now. Don't forget I know yo' ass."

The reverend slid a little closer to Stephanie.

"I know you know me, and I know you. So what are you going to do?"

"What do you mean, what I'ma do?" Stephanie replied. The minister stood up and brushed the dirt from the seat of his trousers.

"Are you going to sit here all day or are you coming with me?"

"Go with you?"

"Yeah, come with me. You don't need to be alone. You need to be with me." He held out his hand to help Stephanie up. She took it and stood, looking extremely concerned.

"Don't look at me like that. Just get in the car."

Stephanie walked around to the passenger side, staring at the reverend the entire time. He traced her every step and opened the door for her. She sat down on the cold leather and he reached in, buckled her seat belt, and kissed her on the cheek very softly.

"I may not be able to take care of you forever, but

you don't have to worry about today." She watched him as he walked around the front of the car. The two never broke eye contact.

"All of your stuff burned up in the fire?" Stephanie nodded. "Let's go get you some things."

He took her to Simply 6 and let her pick out as many clothes as she wanted. *The cheap bastard,* Stephanie thought, *he up in here like he settin' it off and ain't shit in here over ten dollars.*

"Get whatcha want." The reverend followed Stephanie around the store, holding items up to her body. She placed the few pieces of clothing on the counter, he paid for them, and they left.

"You need some shoes, right?"

"Yes," Stephanie replied. The reverend made a quick right into the closest shoe store . . . Payless.

"Payless?" Stephanie looked at him like he was trying her. He returned the awkward stare like *you ain't got shit so you better be happy.*

Even though Stephanie didn't have shit she still had standards. She had every pair of Manolo Blahniks ever made, plus David Yurman, Gucci, Fendi, Prada, and anything that cost money. She'd had them all but everything had burned up in the fire.

"This your size here, ain't it?"

He held up a pair of white patent-leather pumps. "I like these. Get these." As he began to get comfortable with Stephanie he let down his façade and acted like the old John Johnson she knew.

Stephanie rolled her eyes at his country ass and put the shoes back on the rack. But she did manage to find some pairs she could work with. Hell, the store had some straight shit in it.

John paid for the shoes and they went back to the

car. He watched Stephanie with half-open eyes as she pulled down the passenger-side visor and looked at her face. She touched her head, sad about the long weave that Angie had cut off.

"So do you have a place to stay?"

"No, not really. The Red Cross put me up in a hotel but that's only for three days." Stephanie closed the visor and sat back in the seat.

"Which hotel?" The reverend asked, cranking up the car.

"The Holiday Inn on 163rd Street." He drove off toward the hotel.

"You need to clean yourself up. I'ma take you to dinner. It'll take your mind off things. Is that cool?" Remembering Ian, Stephanie nodded. "It's cool," she said.

"Where are you going to stay after the three days are up?"

"I don't know. I don't know what I'ma do."

"Well, we'll work it out. I'll make sure you are taken care of."

The reverend pulled into the parking lot and Stephanie fumbled through her pockets looking for the key to the room. She noticed her cell phone was going dead and she didn't have a charger.

"John, will you buy me a charger for my phone?"

"Sure, no problem. But get cleaned up first." Stephanie found the key and the two entered the room with bags and boxes in hand.

"Thank you for buying those things for me." Stephanie hugged the minister and gave him a kiss on the cheek. He embraced her, bringing her close. The door closed and he locked it.

"Don't mention it. It was nothing."

"Excuse me for a minute." Stephanie went into the

bathroom and shut the door. “I didn’t buy any underwear,” she yelled out, but her words were distorted by the noise of the shower.

The pastor opened the door to the bathroom. “Did you say something?”

Stephanie stood there naked with the water running over her body. She hadn’t closed the shower curtain yet.

The reverend hesitated and looked at her with lusting eyes. “Did you say something?”

Stephanie closed the curtain and repeated, “I didn’t buy any underwear.”

“That’s okay, you won’t need any.” But Stephanie didn’t hear what he said. “Okay, I’ll be out in a second.”

Stephanie leaned her head under the water to shampoo away the dirt and debris from the fight. When she rinsed the soap off her mangled hair and face she opened her eyes to find the pastor standing there butt-naked with a hard dick.

She wiped the water from her face, looked down at his erect penis and calmly spoke.

“It’s not that type of party. I thought you were taking me to dinner.” She reached for a towel to cover her body.

“I am. I just wanna be with you.” He grabbed her hand before she could reach the towel.

“You wanna fuck me, huh?” Stephanie pulled away.

“Yeah, I wanna fuck.” The reverend stroked his penis.

“You really don’t give a shit about me, do you? Our son is dead and you wanna fuck. Besides, you called me all types of whores and bitches and now you want me to give you some? What happened to loose your number? ‘You not fucking with my dumb ass no more.’ What happened to that?” she asked as she began to cry from anger.

“Don’t cry, baby.” The reverend wiped the tears from

her face and leaned toward her as he spoke.

"I didn't mean any of that foolishness." He began to kiss Stephanie very softly on her lips.

"Stop, stop. I don't wanna do this."

"Just give it a minute and it'll feel right. Just give it a minute." The reverend pulled Stephanie close to him, lifting her out of the tub.

"Stop whatcha doin'!"

"You don't need to be alone. I'm just trying to make you feel better." He held Stephanie with one arm and fondled her body with the other.

"Stop!" He wrestled her to the bathroom floor. Her head was pressed against the bottom of the toilet and the preacher was on top of her.

"Stop! Stop!" Stephanie pleaded as he forced her legs apart.

"Just give it a minute and it'll feel right. Relax." He tried to restrain her by holding her arms and putting his chin under her neck.

"Stop!" Stephanie yelled out one last time, but it was too late. He had already inserted himself in her. So she stopped resisting and let him have his way.

He raised himself up and began fucking Stephanie harder and harder.

"I told you it would feel right." He grunted out the words.

Her head was banging against the toilet but she didn't move or talk. She thought of all the times she'd lied to Kevin to see this man and the countless times she had given herself to him freely. For what? His true feelings were finally revealed: he didn't care about her and never had—not to mention Ian. She was just a piece of ass without a face.

The reverend slowed down between each penetrating

thrust and stopped at his highest point, releasing himself inside of her.

Stephanie turned her head to the side and stared at the wall. She couldn't believe that the lie she'd told about the pastor raping her had come to pass. A tear rolled down her face as he removed himself and washed his dick off in the sink.

He looked at her body, bruised from the fight and now molested by him, and watched her as she lay there staring at the wall.

She realized what he had realized just seconds earlier: he might have gotten the pussy but he was about to be fucked. Stephanie turned her head, looking at the pastor from the bathroom floor.

"You raped me," she said in a low, stern voice, with her eyes bulging. "You raped me." She repeated it several times and got louder each time. "You raped me! Look at me." She went into psycho mode. "You beat me up and raped me. You shouldna done this to me. I didn't deserve this. No woman deserves this."

She ran past him and out into the hallway yelling, "He raped me!"

John Johnson panicked and scrambled around trying to find his belongings. He didn't know what to do. He put on his pants, grabbed his shirt and keys, and ran from the room. But he was stopped by hotel security officers, pointing their firearms at his head.

Stephanie was behind them—stark-naked, battered, and bruised--with semen dripping from her vagina. She pointed at him and repeated three words: "He . . . raped . . . me!"

19

Nineteen

Monica and her cousins were still celebrating their beat-down of Stephanie by partying, smoking weed, and drinking cheap liquor.

"That's what family fo'. You gotta let them ho's know." Angie was rolling up a fat blunt and looking at Monica. "We ain't nothing to be fucked with. But fuck all that. Girl, smoke one with yo' family." Monica looked at the four-inch blunt.

"Shit. Whatcha scared?"

"Girl, you know I'm pregnant."

"Shit, this weed. This shit ain't gon' to hurt that li'l muthafucka." Angie pointed at her stomach. "God made this here." She put the unlit blunt under her nose and inhaled deeply. The smell was so strong that she began to choke.

"You see," Angie said, trying to catch her breath, "this is some good shit." The two women in the back of the car agreed.

"Fire that shit up, girl," Monica said, acknowledging that she was willing to smoke.

"That's what the fuck I'm talking 'bout." Angie took

two quick pulls on the blunt, lighting the tip. She extinguished the flame and looked at the end to make sure it was burning evenly, applying a little spit where needed. Then she took one tremendously long drag and when she blew out the smoke, it transferred from her mouth to her nose.

"Damn Snoop, puff puff. Give!" Monica reached for the joint and pulled on it.

"This some good shit." She passed the wet joint to the back seat.

"Damn, I know you needed that. Let that chronic setcha' free." Angie lay back in the seat. She felt like she was melting into the leather.

"Angie!" Monica was in a panic. Her voice cracked when she spoke.

"What's up?"

"I'm feelin' funny. I think I'm bleeding."

"You ain't bleeding, girl. It's the weed that got you trippin'." Angie relaxed as she stared out the window with half-open eyes.

"It's not the weed. I'm bleeding for real. Help me, Angie. What's happening to me?" Monica felt a sticky fluid run down her leg. The blood was flowing profusely and she got hysterical. Angie looked over and saw the blood blackening Monica's clothes.

"Pull over. Hurry up, pull over, girl!" Monica cut across traffic and swerved into a gas station.

"What's wrong with me? What's happening to me?"

"Calm down, Monica. I think you having a miscarriage. Don't trip, we have to get you to the hospital." The two cousins in the back seat were still smoking the joint.

"Put that shit out, you silly bitches. This girl having a miscarriage. One of you ho's got to drive us to the hospital." Monica slid across the seat to Angie and held her, trying to keep her calm.

"I'm not fuckin' up my outfit. You better wipe that blood off the seat."

"Drive, you silly ho'." Nequisha, one of the cousins, put the liquor bag over the blood-drenched seat and reluctantly jumped behind the wheel.

"Turn on the hazards and don't stop at no lights or nothin'. Just drive . . . drive!" Nequisha got behind the wheel and pushed the pedal to the floor.

"What hospital we going to?"

"Jackson, girl. Go to Jackson. Ride out!" Nequisha had all the valves open on the Impala.

"It hurts, Angie. I don't wanna die. What's happening to me?"

"You ain't about to die. Everythang's okay, don't worry."

Blood was flowing out of Monica like a faucet and Angie told Nequisha to hurry. "Keep yo' eyes open."

The women sped down the highway to the hospital and pulled up to Jackson's emergency room. Angie jumped out of the car and ran inside.

"We need a doctor. My cousin bleeding to death."

A nurse near the door walked out to assess the situation. She gave Monica the once-over and signaled for a stretcher. Monica's skin and gums were very pale and the doctors got an IV going immediately.

"What can you tell me about this?" one of the doctors asked, shining a small light into Monica's eyes.

"One minute we was driving and having a good time. The next minute she was yelling she was bleeding. I think she's having a miscarriage or something." The strong stench of weed accompanied every word Angie uttered and the doctor understood exactly what was going on. He and two nurses rushed Monica into one of the rooms.

"Give all her information to the lady at the admissions desk," the nurse told Angie.

When the security doors flew open Angie caught a glimpse of an unexpected face. It was Stephanie sitting on a gurney and having her blood pressure taken. The police were also with her, taking a statement.

Angie panicked and alerted the others. "Yo, Stephanie back there with the police," she said, walking towards the exit. "I'm out this muthafucka!"

"What about Monica?" Nequisha asked as she stood up to leave.

"She where she needs to be. She ah'ight, I can't do shit else for her. I'll call Granny to let her know what's up."

The three women left and Monica was all alone. She was rolled past Stephanie and their eyes fluttered when each saw their nemesis. The encounter was brief because of all the doctors and nurses were attending to Monica.

"Hello, can you hear me?" Monica nodded.

"How many months pregnant are you?" The doctors hurriedly cut away Monica's clothing.

"Sixteen weeks." The doctor pushed on her stomach, feeling for the baby.

"I believe you're much further along than that."

The room was full of new faces and machines.

"What's happening?" Monica asked.

"We're going to do an emergency c-section to try and save your baby."

"But I'm only four months."

"You're more like seven months and you're about to have a baby."

"Where my cousins at? I can't do this by myself." The nurse went out to get Angie, but she and the others had long since fled the scene. So the nurse returned alone, shaking her head.

The doctor prepared to take the baby and the anesthesiologist finished administering the medication. Monica felt weak from all the blood she'd lost and was feeling the effects of the drugs. She spoke slowly and softly. "I can't do this by myself." Then her body went limp and her breathing became very faint. As the nurses continued to prep her the doctor pronounced Monica dead.

Kicking and punching Stephanie had brought on the early delivery. Monica had been so intent on taking Stephanie's life that she'd had no regard for her own.

The doctors focused on saving the baby and immediately took it from Monica. It was only twelve inches long and weighed only six-and-a-half pounds. And it was white.

. . . . .

As Stephanie sat on the gurney, she fell forward into the officers' arms, weeping uncontrollably.

"My baby. My baby. He's alive?" The officer had just given Stephanie the news about Ian. She could not believe it.

"Where is he?"

The officer told her that Ian had apparently run away and ended up at his father's house, Kevin Gray.

"Kevin," Stephanie said softly. She quickly covered her mouth as if she were thinking out loud.

"My baby was with Kevin? But how?"

"We're still trying to sort all of that out. Mr. Gray is being detained for questioning. Your son is on his way here now."

"My baby's coming here? I don't want him to see me like this." Stephanie tried to straighten her clothing. Luckily she had put on one of the outfits the reverend purchased.

"My hair is a mess. I look awful." Stephanie touched

her face, feeling the bruises and swellings.

"You look fine. I'm sure your son won't mind," the officer said.

Stephanie's attention was drawn to the room Monica was in as the doctors began to emerge. When the nurse rolled a baby in an incubator past Stephanie, she looked at what she believed to be Kevin's child. The baby was small and feeble, with tubes running through its entire body. Stephanie waited for Monica to be rolled out as well. She knew they would be transferring her to maternity soon. Twenty minutes passed, but still no Monica.

So Stephanie jumped off the stretcher and walked over to the room Monica was in. There, she was shocked to find Monica's lifeless body covered with a sheet.

"Mommy," a little voice called out. Stephanie turned and looked into Ian's face. She dropped to her knees and held her arms out, reaching for her little boy. Ian ran into her, causing them to tumble to the floor. They embraced and Stephanie kissed Ian all over his face.

As she held him, she looked at Monica's lifeless body one last time and suddenly appreciated her life more. She knew that the dead body could very well have been her own. A small part of her even wished it was.

"I'm so glad to see you. I'm so glad you're okay." She kissed Ian after every word. "You scared me half to death. I don't know what I would have done without you." Stephanie held Ian close and the two hung onto each other.

"What happened to your face, Mommy?" Ian's little eyes began to fill up with water and tears began streaming down his face.

"Mommy had an accident. But I'm okay, baby, don't worry." Stephanie wiped away his tears.

The officer walked over. "Can we give you a lift somewhere, Miss?"

Stephanie's eyes began to shift from side-to-side. She was thinking that she didn't want to take Ian to the hotel but had no choice.

"Yes. Please." Stephanie picked Ian up and his tiny legs wrapped around her waist. Her face reflected all the events of the day. She was not a broken woman, but she was damn close.

They left the hospital with the officers. On the way out she passed an elderly lady with three small children coming into the emergency room. It was Monica's grandmother and kids.

20

Twenty

Word got around about the reverend's arrest. A few of the officers at the station were members of St. Joseph's so it didn't take long before the entire church knew. Everyone's phone was ringing off the hook and the local news station ran the story every thirty minutes. Despite the seriousness of the charges mounted against the pastor, he remained characteristically calm and collected—using his one phone call to reach his lawyer.

"Law offices of Brown and Washington."

"Malcolm Brown, please. This is Reverend Johnson."

"Just a moment." He was put right through because Malcolm was one of the deacons at the church.

"What's up, Reverend? How are you?" Malcolm leaned back in his chair, prepared to hear some uplifting words from his pastor, who frequently called his deacons.

"I'm in jail and I need you to come get me out." Malcolm leaned forward, placing both elbows on his cherry desk.

"You're in jail?"

"Yes. I need you to come get me out," Reverend Johnson repeated in a monotone voice.

Malcolm was shocked and confused. “In jail for what?”

“Sexual assault and battery.”

“What!” Malcolm took off his school-boy glasses. “Where are you? Dade or Broward?”

“I’m at the Dade County Jail.”

“I’m on my way. Don’t say anything! You hear me? Don’t say nothing!”

Malcolm hung up the phone and scrambled around, putting all of his belongings in his briefcase. His secretary buzzed him.

“Yes, Mary.” Malcolm’s tone was rushed.

“Mr. Brown, you have several calls on hold and all of them reference Reverend Johnson.” They were from church members alerting Malcolm about the good reverend’s status.

“Mary, tell everyone I’m out of the office.” Malcolm picked up his briefcase and headed out to the county lock-up.

. . . . .

Back at the police sub-station the cops were still drilling Kevin.

“We know you did something. We just can’t put our fingers on it.”

“A minute ago you knew I committed murder. Now you *know* I did something? Which is it? I killed somebody or I did something else?” Kevin pushed away the pen and pad the detectives had given him to write down his confession to the alleged murder.

“Y’all ain’t got shit and you know it! So you might as well release me.”

“You can forget that! You ain’t going nowhere.” The detectives left the room and two plainclothes cops entered.

"On your feet, Mr. Gray." Kevin stood up.

"What's up now?"

"Turn around." Kevin turned and faced the wall and an officer put leg irons around his ankles.

"You're being transported to County."

"The fuckin' County?" He looked at the cops. Their faces were stony. Then the three left for the jail.

During the ride Kevin was thinking how the County was like a party. He probably knew every fucking body in there. This would just give him an opportunity to catch up with his homies.

"It's hot as a muthafucka back here. Turn up the damn AC!" The glass partition that separated cops from passengers was keeping the AC from circulating in the car. It was at least ninety degrees outside and probably even hotter in the vehicle.

"Let down this fucking window! I'm about to pass the fuck out back here!"

The officers continued talking to each other as if Kevin didn't exist and the thirty-minute ride seemed like an eternity to him. He was overjoyed when they finally reached the jailhouse and thanked the officers when they removed him from the back seat of the patrol car.

"Thank you." He was drenched in sweat. The officers just looked at him. They didn't understand why he thanked them.

Kevin made it to the lock-up just in time to make his first appearance. All the new arrivals, or those needing to see the judge, were shuffled into a large room—the court-house without a court. The judge saw all of the accused via closed- circuit TV. Some impersonal shit.

Kevin looked around and spoke to some of the people he knew. Then his eyes came across someone he believed to be the devil himself--Reverend John Johnson.

"Oh shit! Ain't this a bitch!" Kevin said softly as he looked around to see who else was there. The preacher hadn't made eye contact with Kevin. He was looking around the room like a sick puppy.

Suddenly the preacher's head turned slowly and his eyes fixed on Kevin. His puppy-dog look quickly turned into a fierce stare. John's face was as tight as a drum. His nose was flared and his eyes were locked. Kevin laughed at his futile attempt to recover and look hard.

Kevin mouthed, "You soft-ass bitch, they gon' fuck you." The reverend squinted his eyes to read Kevin's lips so Kevin repeated, "They gon' fuck you!" The reverend understood what was said and re-directed his attention to the bailiff who was calling the first of the inmates to see the judge.

Kevin patiently waited his turn to go before the magistrate. He and John were both eager to find out what the other was in for and just as they were wondering, Kevin's name was called. He walked up to the podium, where a public defender was present to handle his case.

"Mr. Gray, you are charged with murder in the first degree. How do you plead?"

"Not guilty," Kevin responded.

"Hold without bond."

That was it. Kevin didn't have time to open his mouth to say shit. It was a done deal; his ass was staying.

He returned to his seat and waited while ten other inmates were called before Reverend Johnson. Finally the pastor made his way to the podium, where a lanky, nerdy-looking man was waiting. It was Malcolm, the church's attorney.

"Mr. Johnson, you are charged with sexual assault and battery. How do you plead?" Malcolm leaned forward and spoke.

"My client pleads not guilty, Your Honor. Reverend Johnson is a community leader who helps . . ." But Malcolm was cut off by the judge.

"Bail set at one-hundred-fifty thousand dollars." The judge banged his gavel and called the next case.

Kevin translated the sexual assault and battery into common language. "Rape. That muthafucka raping all the ho's," he mumbled under his breath. He didn't know that the pastor had raped Stephanie.

Malcolm was explaining to the reverend the steps they would take to ensure his immediate release. John looked at Kevin with a shitty grin because he would soon be free--back in the comfort of his home and the security of his church. At least that's what he hoped.

The next day Kevin was dressed in orange but he had some unfinished business. He was on the same floor with his homeboy, Clyde.

"What's up, nigga!" Clyde said to Kevin, with his permanent gold teeth showing.

"What's up, bitch!" Kevin responded.

The two were seated directly across from each other and it was the first time they had seen each other since they were at the store.

"Bitch, I know you just didn't call me a bitch. It ain't no guns and razors up in here, my nigga. You know you can't handle me." Clyde bit into an apple and his slobber dripped back into the tray.

"You eatin' a lotta cheese these days. Huh, Clyde."

"Yeah, nigga, I'm a rat . . . you know this. I eat cheese and yo' bitch too." Clyde stuck out his tongue and licked between two of his fingers.

"How's the house?"

"What the fuck you mean, how's the house?" Clyde's eyes went from yellow to fire-engine red.

"I know you didn't burn my shit over a bitch, dawg!"

"It wasn't about the bitch. It was principles involved--a respect thang. You can understand that?"

"Naw, nigga, I can't!"

"Well fuck it then!" The two men stood up at the same time, prepared to rip each other apart, but the correction officers quickly defused the situation.

"I'll see you, my nigga. I'll see you," Clyde said as he walked away.

"See me, then, nigga. See me!"

. . . . .

Three weeks passed and the jail routine was getting monotonous. Kevin spoke to his public defender on several occasions but he didn't know shit and was certainly not trying to help. It didn't matter anyway because the fire inspector had found a gun in the burnt ruble while he was trying to determine the cause of the fire at Clyde's house. He turned the gun over to the police, who ran a ballistics test and found it to be the same gun that killed Ulysses, the junkie. The gun had also been used in several other unsolved crimes--a total of four murders.

No glory, no car chases, and no shoot-outs for Clyde. The state attorney was out to fuck him with a sandpaper dick and he'd never see the streets again. "The rest of your natural-born life," were the judge's exact words.

Kevin was released as soon as the new evidence came to light. On the way out he was escorted past Clyde's cell and saw his old friend crying like a bitch. The worst part of it was that Clyde knew he should have gotten rid of the gun a long time ago. In the end, Clyde fucked himself: he got a life sentence.

Kevin and Clyde looked at each other for the last

time and didn't say a word.

21

Twenty-One

The Red Cross had long ago stopped giving aid to Stephanie and she and Ian had been staying with anyone that would give them a place on the couch or floor. But staying with her stripper-friends was getting old because three and four of them lived together in one-bedroom apartments. Besides, with all Stephanie's money burnt up, they were becoming extremely impatient with her. And on top of that, they all knew the real Stephanie and wanted no part of her crazy ass. So Stephanie called her last home-girl, Jackie.

"Hello."

"Yo girl, what's up?"

"Who this?" Jackie asked, sucking on a chicken bone.

"Stephanie."

"Who?" She wiped meat out of the corners of her mouth.

"Girl stop trippin'. It's me."

"Last I heard, yo' ass was on the run. That dumb-ass nigga, Kevin, came by here looking for yo' stupid ass."

"For real, girl."

"Yeah, that dumb-ass nigga was all up under the bed. All in the attic and shit. You musta' buried that nigga drawers in the backyard or something." Jackie laughed hysterically into the phone and Stephanie returned a fake laugh.

Then, after all the giggling, Stephanie dropped the bomb. "Listen, I need someplace to stay for a minute. I'm ass-out. I need you."

"Umm-hmm, I knew yo' ass wanted something."

"Naw girl. It ain't like that . . ."

"I haven't heard from yo' ass in months. Now you need me."

There was silence. Stephanie didn't say shit. She just waited for Jackie's response.

"You know, I ain't even gon' trip. I'm a true friend."

"Thanks Jackie. We won't be with you long, I promise."

"It's ah'ight girl. Don't say shit else or you might make me change my mind."

"Okay, we'll be there soon."

"What's this *we* shit?"

"Me and Ian."

"I thought that li'l nigga burnt up in the fire."

"Naw, ain't no shit like that happen."

"These ho's know they can tell some lies. Tammy said she saw the nigga on the news or something . . . never mind, fuck it." Stephanie took the phone away from her ear and looked at it.

"Well, we on our way."

"How you gettin' here?"

"The bus."

"Girl it's eleven o'clock in the morning. Where you at?"

"In the Grove."

"In the Grove where?"

"On Charles Terrace."

"By the graveyard?"

"Yeah girl."

"I'll be there in about twenty-five minutes."

"Thanks, Jackie."

"Umm-hmm." Jackie hung up and jumped in her car to pick up Stephanie and Ian.

• • • • •

While his case was pending, the church put the reverend on the back burner and invited guest preachers until they could figure out what to do with his evil ass. And life as the reverend had known it was about to take an even worse turn because the church's advisory board called a meeting to discuss his fate.

"We've called this meeting to discuss the future of St. Joseph's," the lead deacon said as an opener to the Saturday afternoon meeting. "We must consider the future of our community and children." All the deacons and deaconesses amen'd and praised the Lord.

The reverend sat at the head of the huge meeting table with his hands folded and pressed against his mouth.

"Reverend Johnson, we believe it is time for the church to move in a new direction—a direction that does not include you."

The reverend stood up very slowly. But the deacon held out his hand and shook his head. "Before you say anything, we have already put this to a vote." He pointed at the members in attendance.

The reverend looked at each of the fifteen members and most of them were thirty years his senior. They had all watched him grow and a few of them knew him better than he knew himself. That was why they decided to remove him as pastor of the church.

"I can't believe this." The reverend sat back down in his oversized chair.

"I can't believe y'all have voted to remove me from *my* church. My church!"

The board members looked at each other, slightly surprised by his arrogant tone. "This my Daddy church. He built it with his bare hands, but I don't have to remind y'all of that because most of you were here before the church was even built. Y'all can't vote me out. This my church and anything that comes through these doors must have my stamp of approval. I'm the decision maker around here, not y'all. Me, that's who. So you better check the bylaws of the church because I ain't going nowhere!" He sat back in his chair, piping hot. Pissed off that they'd tried him in such a manner.

Just as he was giving them all dirty looks, a thick packet of papers came sliding down from the end of the table under the watchful eyes of everyone present. They followed the packet like spectators at a tennis match until it fell into the reverend's lap.

John Johnson turned the papers right side up. There were the bylaws of the church. And Malcolm, the nerdy lawyer, was the one who had slid the papers down to him. The preacher looked at the documents and put them down on the oak table.

"Huh! So this can't be good for me. Whatcha think, Malcolm?" But Malcolm didn't say anything. He just pushed his school-boy glasses up on his face with his middle finger.

"So, tell me what these papers say," John asked Malcolm.

"On page eleven, refer to Article XVI, Section 6. It says that the governing committee decides who the pastor of the congregation shall be. It also states that the pastor can be removed at any time by the advisory board in the event that he or she displays character unbecoming a minister. And if you look at the last page you will see your signature, acknowledging that you understood and would abide by these laws."

The Reverend looked blank.

"We have voted and it is the decision of this board that you be removed as pastor of the St. Joseph Church. We have decided to give you a severance package so that you can adjust to your new career, whatever that may be. You will also have to seek representation for your upcoming trial because my services are no longer at your disposal."

Malcolm slid an envelope down the table and the reverend opened it. "What's this? This is what I get after all the work and new members I've brought to this church? I developed a radio station, TV ministry, day care, dinner sales, and a K-12 school. And you mean to say that all that is worth a lousy fifty thousand dollars? The church makes that much in a month."

Leander, the head deacon spoke. "You didn't do any of that, boy. The Lord blessed us with those things."

"You self-righteous, ungrateful sons-of-bitches!" The former pastor hocked and spat on the table. "I made this church. Not y'all. Me. And if you think you can get rid of me that fuckin' easy, y'all out y'all fucking mind."

The committee members began leaving the room. Embarrassed at the decision they'd made five years earlier, they realized that John Johnson should never have been the presiding pastor.

"Hold on, this ain't over. The meeting is not over. Where y'all thank y'all going? You can't do this to me. Don't leave! This ain't over."

Then the reverend began to plead with the committee. "Mrs. Mary, you practically raised me." He pulled at the feeble old lady as she pushed herself along with her walker. "Mrs. Mary, don't let them do this to me. Momma Mary, please."

But she turned away and walked past him. And the

others also left. They'd made their decision and it was final.

22

Twenty-Two

Kevin stepped out of jail free as a bird and walked to 12th Avenue, where he waited for the bus. He had thought about calling Plethora to pick him up but didn't feel like going through all the drama. She would probably roll up with her loud-talking, noisy sisters. So he decided to forget about it.

The bus was coming down the street and Kevin stood up and signaled for it to stop. But he didn't have the exact fare and the driver was strictly forbidden to make change, so Kevin had to put a five-dollar bill in the slot for the sixty-cent ride. What else was new? He'd been getting screwed for the past seven months so why should today be different?

The driver handed Kevin about ten transfers and the passengers near the front of the bus snickered. Kevin even heard a little boy remark, "Look at his dumb ass."

He headed to the Hialeah impound yard to retrieve his car, where the police officers told him it had been towed when he was arrested. He'd had eight hundred dollars when he walked into the police station with Ian and he knew he was about to give it up in order to get his car back.

Kevin arrived at the impound yard at 4:58 p.m. There was a lady standing at the front door of the building, but just when he reached the entrance, she flipped the sign on the door so it read "closed."

He started to go off on her but she was inside, where he needed to be, and his car was behind a fifteen-foot wall topped with razor-wire. Four rottweilers roamed the yard. So going off on her was not an option. Kevin knew he could catch more bees with honey than with shit.

"Please, lady. Don't lock up on me. I walked here from the airport. Please let me get my car." Kevin fell to his knees. The woman looked down at him, shaking her head, and momentarily looked away. Then two huge, hairy Latinos appeared out of nowhere and opened the door.

"What's up?"

"Yo playa, I need to get my car up outta here. I walked up here to get it and I ain't got no money for it to be here another day."

"Get off your knees, dawg. Come on in."

The lady said, "I need your ID and pink slip."

"I ain't got no pink slip."

"Give me your ID, then." She took Kevin's ID, punching the numbers into the computer.

"What kind of car is it?

"It's a '74 Chevy." Kevin looked around the lobby while the transaction was being processed.

"Yeah. That'll be $683.73." Kevin paid the lady and she gave him a receipt.

"Juan will bring the car around."

"Thanks, y'all. I really appreciate it."

One man let Kevin out while the other went to retrieve his car. He had to check himself because he had just thanked them for taking nearly seven hundred dollars of his money.

"Fuck it," he said as the car rolled out from behind the monster gate. The guy got out of the car, leaving the door open.

"Yo, hold up!" Kevin said as he began to search under the seat and in the glove compartment. "Where the fuck my CD's?"

He popped the trunk to see if his music was still there and Juan managed to slip back into the yard behind the massive wall. Kevin's trunk was clean. Wasn't shit back there except the spare tire. He walked back to the entrance of the yard and pounded on the door.

"Hey, you thieven muthafuckas!" He banged on the door repeatedly. Finally Juan came to see what all the commotion was about.

"What's up?" Juan asked from behind the door.

"Where all my shit at?"

"What shit?"

"Muthafucka, don't play with me. You know what the fuck I'm talkin' 'bout." Kevin pointed toward the car. "Where my CD's and speakers at?"

"I don't know whatcha talkin' about. When we towed the car it was like it is now. Just like it is now."

"That's bullshit and y'all know it! Y'all clipped a nigga."

Kevin calmed himself. He looked down at the ground with his hands on his hips. "You know I ought to do something to all three of you bitches. But I ain't gon' even trip. You got it." Kevin walked off, got in his car, and drove away.

He rolled down the window to take in the fresh air of freedom--then reached into the glove compartment to retrieve a Black and Mild.

"Fuck!" he yelled out and hit the oak steering wheel. "They stole them too."

. . . . .

Kevin arrived at his apartment hoping to find everything intact. But when he opened the door he was overwhelmed by the stench of rotten food and mold. He had been away long enough for the electricity to be turned off.

He picked up the phone, checking for a dial tone. It was still working and the double beeps alerted him to the fact that he had new messages. Most of them were from his homeboys, wondering what was up. But the last message was from Monica's big cousin, Angie. She explained that Monica had died in childbirth, and that he could come to Jackson's maternity ward to see their new son.

Instead of mourning Monica's death, Kevin was pissed because he knew that the baby wasn't his. Typical Monica . . . playing games to the bitter end. Another problem he had to face.

But he was happy to be out of jail and knew that the real work would begin. What about Ian? And Stephanie? With Monica, at least the drama was over. Then his thoughts shifted to his childhood friend, Clyde, who was never going to see the streets again. And as for punk-ass Reverend Johnson, he had to keep an eye open for that fool.

Kevin sat in his chair, running these thoughts through his head in an attempt to sort them out and deal with them. He sat in the hot apartment, contemplating his next move.

After several hours, Kevin was still thinking of a plan of action. Then he realized that he didn't need a plan because everything was already done. The only thing that mattered was Ian, and he was gone. He also realized that Stephanie had never loved him and that he was no longer safe on the streets: Clyde had been his enforcer and once the word got out that he'd had something to do with Clyde's situation, Clyde's homeboys were going to come for him. As for Monica, she didn't fit into any of the thoughts, and fuck everybody else.

Kevin decided he was going to cut his losses and bounce to Atlanta. He had a cousin there who had been begging him to relocate.

"Fuck it!" Kevin said out loud. He stood up, stretched, and decided he would leave for Atlanta that very night. After packing his shit in a huge duffle bag, he looked at the stereo equipment and nice furniture and decided to leave it all.

He jumped into the shower but the water was cold because the electricity had been turned off. So he hurried to finish up and get out of town. But just as he turned off the water the phone rang . . .

. . . . .

Stephanie was posted up over Jackie's house. Her new nigga was a female and Jackie was treating her like a piece of meat.

"Go put on the outfit I got you." She slapped Stephanie on the ass.

"Stop, Jackie. You know Ian is up."

"What the fuck that gotta do with anythang? Get in there and put on what I told ya." Jackie had Stephanie under lock-and-key. She was more jealous and possessive than any man Stephanie had ever encountered and Stephanie was at an extreme disadvantage. She knew how to handle men but found it difficult to handle Jackie. Strangely, that turned her on.

"When you puttin' him back in school?" Jackie was face-to-face with Stephanie, helping her remove her clothing.

"Next week. I just don't want him to go to the same school. The other kids may pick on him or give him a hard time."

"Send him to a private school. They got vouchers for that private shit." Jackie rubbed her hands across Stephanie's breast as she moved her fingers in and out of her slowly. "Kiss me."

The two women lip-locked and exchanged saliva. Then Jackie got the rubber cock out of the night-stand and strapped it on tightly.

"You know what's up, so don't even look like that." Stephanie reluctantly grabbed the nine-inch, neon penis and squeezed firmly. "Suck my dick!" Jackie put her hand on Stephanie's shoulder and guided her to the floor. Stephanie grabbed a pillow off the bed and placed it under her knees. Jackie rubbed--then slapped--the penis across Stephanie's lips.

"Put your hands down. Let me do it." Jackie didn't want any help from Stephanie. "Open your mouth." Jackie pushed the cock into Stephanie's mouth until her forehead touched her stomach. Then she pulled back slowly, humping Stephanie's face.

"Stand up." Stephanie stood up and the two began to kiss. Then Jackie turned Stephanie around and began kissing her on the neck and upper back. She reached around, fondling Stephanie's vagina.

"Bend over." Jackie inserted the penis in Stephanie and pushed herself up against Stephanie's buttocks. Jackie moved vigorously in and out, and from side-to-side. Stephanie was blowing and making huffing noises. Jackie sucked on her thumb, soaking it with saliva before sticking it in Stephanie's rectum.

Then Jackie removed the dildo and pushed

Stephanie down onto the bed. She snatched off the cock-strap and lay on top of Stephanie, forcing her tongue into Stephanie's mouth.

"Close your eyes." Jackie lay on top of Stephanie's naked body, grinding and pumping. She moved down to her breast, sucking one and pinching the other. Then she put her pinky inside Stephanie and wiggled it slowly. Stephanie began to move and slide slowly away from the tickling finger but Jackie followed it with her tongue, sucking Stephanie's clitoris.

They were interrupted by three soft knocks on the bedroom door.

"Momma." It was Ian.

"Yes, baby." Stephanie said, holding Jackie's head on her pussy. "What is it?"

"I'm hungry."

"I'm cuming, baby."

Ian walked away from the door.

Jackie took her mouth away from Stephanie and watched her body shake as she climaxed.

"I made you feel good, baby?"

"Umm-hmm." Stephanie replied, licking her lips.

Jackie took off the oversized t-shirt, exposing her less-than-perfect body. "Get up." Jackie lay down on the bed and moved Stephanie out of the way. She opened her vagina and began sucking her own breast. Then she pulled herself back, exposing the little man in the boat. The sea was juicy but milky.

"Come get it." Stephanie almost threw up at the sight. She was living foul and she knew it. But with no place to go and no one else to turn to, she soaked her face in Jackie's overly juicy tunnel of love.

"Slow down." Jackie pushed Stephanie's head away. "Slow down. Take yo' time." Jackie rubbed the side of

Stephanie's face and Stephanie rested her chin on Jackie's vagina. "Lick me slow."

The doorknob turned and Ian came in the room. "Momma, I'm hungry . . ." He stood there in shock, unable to make sense of what he was seeing.

"Get out! Close the door!" Stephanie yelled, wiping her glistening lips. Ian turned and ran, leaving the bedroom door open.

"Ian." Stephanie leaped up and went after her son.

"Come back here! You just gon' leave me like this?" Jackie was sprawled across the bed. "You got your nut; I want mine. He ah'ight, he already seen us. You can explain it to him later. We'll both explain it. Come finish what you started. He'll be ah'ight. Come 'ere, he'll be ah'ight." Stephanie realized she had met her match. Jackie was even more selfish and heartless than she was.

She knew she should attend to her child but she couldn't make herself move and just stood in the doorway, looking down the hall. Then she looked back at Jackie and slowly closed the door, leaving Ian alone to sort out his traumatic experience.

Ian ran into the bathroom crying. He plundered through Stephanie's purse and threw her things on the floor. When he found her cell phone he dialed the only number he had committed to memory: Kevin's. The phone rang . . .

. . . . .

Kevin stepped out of the shower slightly chilled and looked at the ringing phone. He walked hesitantly towards it, put his hand on the receiver, and picked it up slowly. Water dripped from his raised elbow.

"Hello."

"Daddy!"

"Ian? What's wrong, boy? Where you at?" Ian was crying into the phone and his words were slurred and difficult to understand. "Ian, Ian. Calm down, son. Calm down, what's wrong?" Kevin pressed the phone hard against his ear. "Say it slow son, say it slow."

"Momma."

"Momma what?"

"I saw Momma with her head between Jackie's legs."

"Wait a minute. Say that again. Daddy needs for you to stop crying and speak calmly into the phone."

"I saw Momma and she had her head between Jackie's legs."

"Did they have on clothes?"

"No, they didn't have on clothes, Daddy."

Kevin was furious. He was pacing frantically back and forth.

"Where you? Is you at Jackie's house?" His speech was as erratic as his feelings. He stuck his fist in his mouth to stop from cursing and his teeth sank in so far that drool and blood ran down his arm.

"Why the hell all my stuff on the floor?" Stephanie burst into the bathroom where Ian was cowering. "What the hell you doing with my phone?" She snatched the phone away from him and Ian braced himself to absorb any blow she might throw. But Stephanie just gave him an unforgiving look and raised the phone to her ear.

"Who the fuck is this?"

"Bitch, I know you ain't over that bitch Jackie house bumpin' pussy in front of my boy."

"Oh, look who fresh out of jail and trying to play daddy. Muthafucka, don't worry about what the fuck I'm doing. I know all your fucking business and I'll have the feds over there looking for yo' monkey ass."

But by then Stephanie was talking to herself. “Hello, hello . . . hello.” There was no answer. So Stephanie hung up and turned her attention to Ian.

“What did you tell him?” Stephanie had him by the shoulders, sinking her nails into his skin. “What did you say!” Stephanie shook him violently.

“What the hell all this damn yelling about!” Jackie walked into the bathroom stark naked.

“Ian called Kevin.” Stephanie looked into Ian’s eyes as she spoke. “Why did you do that?”

“I hate you and I hate being here. I want to be with Daddy.” Ian broke away from Stephanie and ran to the room he was staying in.

“Let that little nigga go and stay with Kevin. Fuck, that little muthafucka just gettin’ in the way of what I’m feeling,” Jackie said as she stuck her tongue in Stephanie’s ear.

“What you think Kevin gon’ do? Ian was just on the phone with him. Ain’t no telling what he told him. I was talking to him and the nigga just hung up the phone. He didn’t say shit. He just hung up.”

“He ain’t gon’ do shit! Y’all ho’s give them niggas too much power over y’all. He ain’t nothing but some dick and balls. What the fuck he gon’ do?”

Jackie stood there with a smirk on her face. “That nigga ain’t gonna do shit but fuck around and go back to jail he come ’round here fuckin’ with me.” She sashayed her fat, lumpy ass down the hall to the kitchen. “Don’t worry about shit, that nigga ain’t gon’ do nothing.”

But Stephanie knew better. She knew Kevin. Moreover, she knew Ready.

Stephanie went into Ian’s room. He was lying on the bed face down, crying his eyes out. She sat down beside her son and rubbed his back softly before she spoke.

"Ian, baby, I'm sorry. Mommy didn't mean to hurt you. You know I love you." Ian shook from her touch. For the first time, he was afraid of her and what she might do to him.

"All that li'l nigga need is a ass-whippin'." Jackie stood in the doorway eating a mango. "He don't know his place. A child has to stay in they place. That's why don't none of my kids stay here. They don't know how to stay in their place."

Stephanie turned and looked at Jackie with fearless eyes. "This my child. You need to stay in yo' place."

Jackie sucked on the mango seed and just looked at Stephanie, sizing her up before she spoke. "I tell you what. You get yo' shit and that li'l bastard and get the fuck up out my house. I don't like how yo' pussy taste no way." She threw the mango seed at Stephanie.

Stephanie thought about fighting Jackie, but knew it was a no-win situation. Jackie was too big and burly for her to stand a chance.

"We'll leave!" Stephanie stormed out of the room and gathered the few things she had. She put them and Ian's belongings in a garbage bag. But she began to move slower and slower as she realized she had no place to go.

Jackie knew it too. She just put her oversized t-shirt back on and sat on the edge of the bed, laughing as she watched Stephanie walk back and forth.

"Sit yo' silly ass down. Where you gonna go? You ain't got no place to go. Stop frontin'."

Stephanie knew she was right. She was ass out--up the creek in a boat with no paddle.

"Come here." Jackie motioned for Stephanie. She walked over and stood between Jackie's legs. "Why you trippin'?" But before Stephanie could answer there were four loud knocks on the front door.

23

Twenty-Three

Kevin was outside knocking on the door like the ATF, except he banged even harder than they did. Finally, he kicked.

"I know you ho's hear me. Open this muthafuckin' door!" Stephanie panicked and jumped in the closet.

"It's Kevin," she said in a petrified voice.

"Who the fuck is Kevin? He don't run shit around here. This my damn house." Jackie wobbled to the front door.

"Who the fuck is it?"

"Bitch, open this door!" The door swung open violently and obscenities flew out of Jackie's mouth. She was known for fighting men and winning.

"Don't be coming over here bangin' on my door 'bout to tear the muthafucka down. Who the fuck you 'posed to be? 5-0?" Kevin punched Jackie dead in the mouth, leveling her.

"Shut up bitch!" He shook his hand and checked his fist for teeth marks.

"Ian! Ian!" Kevin yelled out, searching through the house. Ian emerged from the room, running towards Kevin with open arms.

"Daddy, Daddy." But his path was cut off by Stephanie.

"What the fuck are you doing?" Stephanie muttered as she looked past Kevin and saw Jackie's motionless body on the floor.

"What are you doing?"

"Don't ask me what I'm doing. Just give me Ian." Ian struggled to break away from Stephanie. "Give him to me. Look at the life you living. He don't need to grow up seeing this."

"Look at your life! Like it's much better than mine. You a drug dealer, Kevin. You kill people--if not with a gun--then definitely with the dreams you selling."

"I gave all that up. I'm leaving for Atlanta tonight and starting my life over. I wanna take Ian with me. He deserves a chance at life but not like this."

But Stephanie held onto Ian tightly. "He's all I got. He's the only thing I got in the world that's mine." She began to cry and dropped to one knee, hugging Ian. Kevin thought, *everything in Stephanie's life came down to having control and gaining possessions. Even as an adult, she hadn't learned that human beings weren't possessions that could be bartered and sold. Stephanie loved Ian, but even more than that, she loved having something to call her own.*

"I know you love him, Stephanie. I love him too. And he can't grow up like this." Kevin gestured around the room and pointed at Jackie, who was coming to. "Let me have him--let me at least try. Give him a chance. Give our son a chance."

Stephanie slowly released Ian and he ran to Kevin with open arms. But Kevin suddenly felt a sharp pain across the back of his neck. And then everything went black.

. . . . .

He woke up with a splitting headache and his hands and feet bound. He blinked several times, trying to focus. Then he felt a warm fluid on his face. It was the former Reverend John Johnson pissing on him.

"Wake up bitch!" Kevin shook his head and turned to the side to shield himself from the urine. He rolled over and focused on Jackie and Stephanie, who were sitting on the couch in the living room--not moving. Then he managed to look up and see the most ungodly image standing over him.

"You know what time it is?" The reverend slowly walked around Kevin in a circle. "It's payback time."

Reverend Johnson threw a broken broomstick next to Kevin. Then he bent down and rolled him over so he could look death in the face. The preacher cocked the hammer back on the small .380 and put it to Kevin's head.

"Because of y'all I lost everything I worked so hard to build. Because of you I ain't got shit. I lost my church, I lost the respect of the community, and I lost my power." With each word he pushed the gun harder and harder against Kevin's head. "I'ma make sure you pay! But you gon' suffer first." He spat in Kevin's face and shoved him back to the ground, putting his foot on his chest.

"And as fo' your dry, pussy-triflin' ass," the reverend added as he pointed the gun at Stephanie, "you were the worst fucking thing that ever happened to me." Then he swung the gun toward Jackie, who was suffering from what appeared to be a dislocated jaw. "You just in the right place at the wrong time. All y'all gon' meet y'all maker tonight."

"What about the boy?" Kevin said from the floor. But Johnson just put his foot on Kevin's throat, applied pressure, and laughed as he looked at Ian. .

"Somebody gotta tell the story. Get up!" He motioned for Stephanie to move off the couch and she walked reluctantly towards him. John grabbed her by the back of her head and pushed her down next to Kevin.

"Take his clothes off!" The reverend stood over the two with the gun trained on Kevin. "Hurry up! Take that shit off!"

Then he bent down and picked up the broken broomstick. "I'ma give you a little history lesson before I shove this stick up yo' ass. Back in the day, the slave master would take one of the strongest slaves and parade him around the yard for everyone to see. Once he had the crowd of slaves gathered, you know what they would do?" He pushed his foot harder against Kevin's throat. "Do you know what they would do? Blink once for no and twice for yes." Kevin blinked once. "They would rape him in front of all the other men, women, and children. You know why?" he looked down at Kevin. "Blink, muthafucka!" Kevin blinked once. "Because they wanted to break him. How can a man that has been fucked by another man be respected by his woman, his children, or his peers. I'ma break you, boy."

The reverend looked at Kevin and spoke very slowly. "First I'ma loosen you up with this stick. Then I'ma fuck you myself—right in front of this bastard and these bitches."

Kevin's eyes widened at the words. "Yeah, that's the same look I had on my face just before you sodomized me."

"You crazy, John, you crazy." Stephanie stood up. She had finished removing Kevin's pants.

"Sit the fuck down and watch." Stephanie shook her head as the reverend unzipped his pants.

"No, you can't do this!"

"Bitch, you can't stop me. After I fuck him in his ass, I'ma fuck you in yours. Oh, but I forgot you like that freaky shit."

Stephanie rushed him, running into him and reaching for the gun. Jackie jumped up and fled the house.

Stephanie was struggling with the preacher but he was too strong and Kevin could only watch helplessly from the floor. He tried to kick the man but his attempts were futile.

Suddenly, though, the preacher felt a little more resistance on his arm. It was Ian, fighting to free his mother from the reverend's grasp. But John Johnson flung the two off with a rush of strength and let out a loud yell.

The yell, however, was overshadowed by a round of gunfire. Everyone froze and no one took a breath.

Kevin looked up at the reverend, who seemed to be in shock as he looked at Stephanie. Her eyes were fixed on Ian because he was staring at her without blinking.

"Ian!" Stephanie screamed, crawling to her son. Kevin turned his head to look at the boy and the preacher just stood there, stuck.

"Ian!" Stephanie grabbed Ian's lifeless body. She was yelling uncontrollably. "Ian, Ian. Not my baby, not my baby." She sat there, rocking him back and forth.

The reverend looked at the horrific scene and bolted for the door. Kevin yelled out in anguish, bound and helpless.

Kevin lay face down, looking at Ian while his mother held him in her arms. The boy's eyes were still open and a single tear fell from his tiny face.

Jackie came back and managed to call the police. But it was too late. Ian was gone--for real this time.

. . . . .

Originally, John Johnson had staked out Kevin's house so he could kill him when he got the chance. When Kevin left home the pastor had followed him—not realizing that he was on his way to see Stephanie.

Once there, however, the reverend's mouth had begun to salivate because he thought he could kill two birds with one stone. But when his murder scene didn't go as planned, he fell deeper into his insanity.

Running out of Jackie's house he whipped his white Cadillac through the streets of Miami, bent on getting to St. Joseph Church.

He arrived at the church to find all the locks changed. It enraged the deranged man even more and he got into his car and backed up clear across the parking lot. Then he grabbed the wheel with both hands, punching the V-8 engine. The car let out an enormous roar and its tires screamed, struggling trying to bite the pavement. When the rubber finally met the road, the car took off like a rocket and crossed the forty yards in a flash, plowing into the church and wrecking everything in its path. The enormous doors broke into pieces from the impact.

The pastor was saved from serious injury by the car's air-bags, though they they did remove part of the skin from his face.

The Cadillac's engine was still racing because the reverend's foot was pressed against the pedal. He pushed the air-bag down and took his foot off the gas. Then he got out and stood there for a moment, listening to the church's alarm blaring.

Running over to the control panel, he quickly punched in some numbers. It was just his luck that they hadn't changed the security code.

Then he pulled out his cell phone and dialed the TV

station, identifying himself and alerting them to what he'd just done. He also told them that if they hurried, they could witness the greatest show on earth.

He hung up and made his way to the utility closet where all the tents were stored. Grabbing the spikes that were used to hold the tents in place--as well as a miniature sledge-hammer--he made his way to the podium where he used to lead the church. He looked out at the empty seats.

The car's headlights were shining directly on him, casting a shadow on the wall. He turned his head and looked at the enormous cross behind the pulpit. Crawling over twelve rows of pews, he rubbed his hands across it.

"They talked about Jesus and he was the Son of God. I want them to talk about John because I'm God's child too."

He took one of the spikes out and drove it through his hand. Then he looked at the hammer in his hand and realized he couldn't crucify himself. So he pulled the spike from his hand, screaming and shaking from the excruciating pain.

"The wages of sin are death!" he screamed out repeatedly, running through the church to the storage closet. He removed the ropes and ran upstairs to the balcony of the church, tied the rope so it made a tight noose around his neck, and tied the other end around the balcony pews that were bolted to the floor. As he began to feel faint from all the blood he had lost, he stepped up on the rail, ready to take his leap of faith. He swayed back and forth like a boat in rough water.

The sound of sirens and helicopters woke him from his drunken state. News cameras and cops made their way into the church through the huge whole left by the car.

When the reverend saw the lights flashing from the TV crews, he leapt from the balcony, speaking in tongue, and stopped just short of the floor. His neck had snapped. Reverend Johnson twitched and jerked as the cameras broadcast the event live across the tri-county area.

24

Twenty-Four

A week later it was time to lay Ian's body to rest. Kevin awoke at dawn and sat up in bed, not wanting to start his day. He thought about how you never knew what each new day would bring or how it would end. A week ago he had been arguing with Chicos about a stolen sound system. Now he was laying his boy to rest.

Starting the day would mean having to begin getting dressed for Ian's funeral so he stayed in bed. Besides, dawn was Kevin's favorite time of day: the events of the previous day were washed away and the possibilities of a new one arose with the sun. Dawn was also the time his clients settled in from their night-crawling, and the ones who managed to function on the poison would go back to their families and jobs. As for the other folks, they were still asleep and happily unaware of whatever disappointments they might face before sunset.

Kevin tried to drift back to sleep, but the last seven months intruded on his thoughts. Stephanie--his beloved--had turned out to be his greatest despair. She had never loved him; she had only loved the life she thought he could provide. And when he couldn't deliver, she'd moved on to someone who could. Kevin thought, *they say death comes in threes. There was Monica, the reverend, and now Ian.*

Everything in him wished that Stephanie had been among those three—not their pure, innocent son. The thought that she had been granted even one more day on earth made him sick.

On his way to the bathroom he saw that the sun had come up and knew it was time to say a final farewell to the real warrior in his twisted life. He remembered that he'd told Ian not to cry for any man when they were at the police station and knew he'd now have to heed his own words. Could he really be *Ready* for whatever?

The hours seemed to fly by and the two o'clock funeral was only thirty minutes away. Kevin put the final touches on the only suit he would ever buy—an all-black, Sean John, two-piece, with a matching shirt and tie.

But he had to push himself to go out the door because he couldn't stop blaming himself for Ian's death. He chose to forego the services at the church, knowing that most people attended only to be nosy.

Kevin arrived at the grave-site late. He moved through the gathering of mourners and put his hand on the closed casket, shutting his eyes and giving thanks for the short time he'd had with Ian.

Looking past the small casket that held the boy he knew as his son, he saw the woman he had believed he wanted to spend the rest of his life with. She was wrapped in Jackie's arms.

Kevin was sickened. He had learned more about Stephanie than he cared to know and was sure she would only be with Jackie until the "slip-and-fall" money ran out. He wished he never had to deal with her or see her again.

Stephanie stared at Kevin and he knew she blamed him for everything. One day he was going to have to deal with her crazy ass. But today was not that day.

Kevin stepped away from the casket and listened to the minister saying his few words. Then Ian's body was lowered into the ground.

Kevin cried for his son. He cried because he missed him. And he cried because Ian would not get to live the new life Kevin had planned for both of them. He knew that he only had one time to get it right. *One life, no sequel,* he thought to himself.

Kevin walked away from the burial site and from his entire ghetto fabulous lifestyle. He decided to head directly to Atlanta, leaving behind the expensive furniture he and Stephanie had picked out—and, most importantly--memories of her.

He jumped in his box Chevy and drove away from the grave as Stephanie's eyes followed the car.

Tomorrow was not promised to Kevin, but tomorrow was all he had to look forward to. He rolled down the windows so the wind would blow away his tears.

One Life No Sequel
Tomorrows Not Promised

Group Questions To Ponder . . .

We invite your reading group the unique opportunity to discuss the following questions to enhance your reading expereince. As always, Michael Gainer sends much love to each of you.

Enjoy!

Discussion Questions

1. Describe Kevin. How do you as the reader see him?

2. Would you sell drugs or strip to support your family?

3. If Kevin had met a different type of woman, would he have eventually left the hustle game?

4. Was Kevin evil?

5. What advice would you give Kevin to answer some of the question he had in his head?

6. Did Stephanie ever care about Kevin?

7. Why do you think Stephanie was the way she was?

8. Do you think Ian's life would have been better with Kevin in Atlanta?

9. What were Stephanie's intentions with Clyde?

Discussion Questions

10. Is Jackie the perfect mate for Stephanie?

11. Was Reverend Johnson misleading the church, or was he the victim?

12. Should a man have love and concern for a child that he found out was not his?

13. If you were Monica, would you have terminated the pregnancy?

14. Why do you think Monica decided to keep the child?

15. Do circumstances determine the type of person you are?

You thought *Dumb As Me* Was It . . . It Was Only The Beginning!

COMING SOON . . .

Another
Michael Gainer
Novel

SON OF A ROOSTER

The Prequel To *Dumb As Me*

A Preview . . .

Chapter One

My punk-ass daddy, Henry Drake, was just the dick I rode in on. I called him “the Rooster” because he always strutted around the house with his chest out. Talked shit all day long but made the most noise early in the morning. And like any rooster, tried to fuck every hen he could.

The Rooster was a tall, slender man, about six foot four and two hundred twenty pounds. His skin was very bright and his hair was naturally red. He had funny-colored eyes too. They changed with his mood: green when he was happy and gray when he was angry. I can count the times I saw them gray.

My old man grew up at a time when being a bright-skinned brother had its advantages. And trust me, he used it to the extreme.

He grew up in a God-fearing home. My grandparents lived by the words in the bible, but Henry was cut from a different cloth: his heart was set on being the biggest entertainer on the planet.

He grew up singing in the church choir and eventually formed a band with some of the other boys in the neighborhood, sneaking out to practice after his parents were asleep. Henry often told stories about how they rehearsed and copied the moves of the Motown groups until they came up with their own.

They got paying jobs, playing local gigs and clubs, and were eventually discovered at a talent show hosted by a major radio station. They won first place and were awarded a recording contract. That was his dream, and all Henry's hard work and dedication seemed like they were about to pay off.

He only had one problem: The preacher's sixteen-year-old daughter was knocked up and he was the father. So Henry had a choice. He could go with the band or marry my mother. But the choice was easy for him because it was not his to make. He was forced to marry my mother and raise his unborn seed. Forced to be a man and forget about his childhood dreams. My grandfather was going to see to that.

My grandfather was a white man and he and the Rooster looked just alike. He was a carpenter by trade and always wore flannel shirts and overalls no matter what the weather.

Henry tried to explain to my grandfather that he could make more money from his music than from any job but my grandfather thought that was nonsense. "Dreams are for fools," were his exact words.

So the group had to forget about its big break. The Rooster was the voice and without the voice there was no group.

My father tried to recapture some of the fame by playing locally but he blamed my mother for his lack-luster career. And he blamed me for being born--telling me he wished I was a blow-job. He always complained that everyone was holding him back but I never heard him blame himself.

"Justin." My father called my name loudly and forcefully.

"Yes sir," I answered quickly, moving toward his voice. It seemed that my little eight-year-old legs were not moving fast enough. I turned the corner, rushing into the kitchen, and stumbled from the heavy load of books on my back.

"Yes sir."

"Boy, what are you doing?" My father paused briefly after every word.

"Getting ready for school." He looked at me from head-to-toe, sucking on a pork chop bone.

"Tuck your shirt in, boy."

"Yes sir." I hurried to put my shirt inside my trousers and was careful to align the shirt, belt, and pants.

"Sit down and eat breakfast with your father." The Rooster looked at my mother, who was busy at the stove. She cooked breakfast for my father every morning, even if he wasn't home. She didn't want him to walk in when there was no food on the table. Often it went un-eaten.

Both of my parents talked about their lives so much that I knew the stories backward and forward. My mother, Sylvia Drake, was the daughter of Pastor Ben Prince. She was his pride and joy and he'd often refer to her during his his sermons, using her as the ideal of how a little girl should be: sugar, spice, and everything nice. She would sit in the front pew, dressed in white with pink lace, and her hair was always in candy-curls.

Yes, she was daddy's little girl until she begin to vomit in the morning and her stomach bulged slightly from the baby growing inside. She told me that the situation really got interesting when it came out that she was pregnant by the skinny, red kid who sang in the choir. That's when all hell broke loose. My grandfather forced her to move out of the house and she lived with Henry and his parents for a few months until they tied the knot.

Henry was forced to turn his part-time hobby--cutting hair--into a full-time job. Even after she married, her father wouldn't speak to her, and he doesn't to this day.

My mother never had a chance to be her own person. She just went from the hold of her father, the preacher, into the grip of the devil himself, the Rooster.

I saw my mother as a beautiful woman. She had the kind of beauty other women complimented. But all the years of dealing with Henry eventually took their toll on her stunning looks. She stopped considering herself pretty and often said she was ugly.

Those weren't her words, though. That was Henry talking. He always belittled her and put her down but she was not the woman he tried to make her. She was capable of anything and the concepts and ideas she shared with me still amaze me. She could see and do things that others could only imagine.

She only had one flaw: The Rooster. He was like a virus; she couldn't shake him. No matter how many times he mistreated, beat, and disrespected her, she couldn't bring herself to leave him. She believed she was ruined for all other men and she probably was, because I later learned that Henry had given my mother herpes. I think that's why she put up with so much of his shit. She was foolish enough to believe that no other man would give her the respect she was due.

I would often sit and look at my mother with black-and-blue marks on her arms and face from where Henry had beaten her. I don't know why he didn't just leave her. He was fucking nearly every woman he saw, or at least he tried to.

My mother told me that my father was the only man she had ever been with. And I know that the only mistake she ever made was loving the wrong man.

"Sylvia," the Rooster called out to my mother.

"Yes baby," she answered, nervous about what he might say.

"Fix this boy a plate." My mother had cooked pork chops, grits, eggs, and homemade biscuits with sugar-water. My father would only drink sugar-water in the morning because he said it made him strong.

My mother put the plate down on the table and rubbed the top of my head before she spoke. "Eat all of your food so you can grow up big and strong like your father." She knew I didn't want to be anything like the bastard. I sat across from him looking at him with my nostrils flared. I hated him even as a child.

"Why you looking at me like that, boy?" My mother stopped moving and looked at me. She called my name softly while my father stared at me.

"Justin, don't look at your father like that."

"Shut up!" he said. "I know what's wrong with you, boy. You thinking about what you saw last night." He leaned back in his chair and laughed, grabbing his crotch.

Yeah, he was right. I *was* thinking about what I saw. I had been awakened by strange noises and had gone into my parents' room. The Rooster was making love to my mother and he just looked me in the face and smiled. He didn't mind me being there. He didn't mind me watching.

My mother was moaning and he was covered with sweat. The Rooster finished his business, grunting as he rammed himself inside her. Then he got up and walked over to me. My mother pulled the sheet over her to cover her naked body. And the Rooster closed the door in my face.

"Don't worry, boy, you'll get you some pussy soon. I

got my first piece of pussy when I was nine years old." My mother cringed.

"Henry!" My mother called out my father's name. He turned his head slowly, looking at her.

"You got something to say?" He put his fist on the table. My mother looked at his hands and said, "No, it's just time for Justin to catch the bus." She shuffled me out the door but I eye-balled my old man the entire time. I hated how he treated her. Shit, I hated how he treated me. I used to pray at night that I would wake up a grown man so I could whip his ass.

"Try and get you some pussy!" he said, just before my mother closed the door.

.....

One of the few outlets we had was the church. My mother lost herself in it. She believed that she could pray enough for my father to change him from the heartless muthafucka he was. Hope was the only thing she had to hold onto. She hoped he would love, cherish, and be faithful to her like he had promised when they married, but it was a pipe-dream. He was hopeless. They were both hopeless and I was caught up in the middle of all of their fuckery.

My mother and I usually stayed in church all day on Sunday. She taught Sunday school, sang in the choir, and cooked dinners at the church. We were always there from sunrise to sunset.

But one Sunday she wasn't feeling well and decided to go home. She had been vomiting uncontrollably.

"What's wrong, Momma?"

"Momma doesn't feel too good, baby. We're going to leave." It was the first time in the history of my going to church that the good Sister Drake was going to leave early. And it was just before the morning service concluded. She cranked up the Monte Carlo and we made the ten-minute trip home.

"Are you going to be okay?"

"Yes, I'm going to be just fine." She drove a little while before she spoke again. "Justin."

"Yes, Momma."

"I'm going to have a baby."

"You are!"

"That's why I've been so sick lately." She grabbed my hand and squeezed it softly. "Baby, do me a favor."

"Sure. Anything, Momma."

"Don't mention this to your father."

"Okay, Momma. I won't say a word."

We pulled up to the house. The Rooster's car was parked in the driveway. That damn heathen didn't ever go to church, not even on Easter Sunday.

My mother opened the front door. We walked in and were surprised by what we saw. Henry was making love to Ms.Parker. She lived up the street and was supposed to be one of my mother's closest friends.

Momma began to vomit at the sight of my father fucking Ms. Parker. The Rooster walked out of the room naked, leaving the door open. His dick was still wet.

"I thought y'all was going to be in church all day." He went into the kitchen and got two beers out of the refrigerator.

"How could you do this to me?" My mother was crying hysterically. "You don't love me. You can't love me and do me like this."

"I love you, baby, but this ain't got nothing to do with you. This about me. Now you go ahead and go back to church. We'll act like none of this ever happened. Go on now." He pushed Momma toward the door.

"What! Act like this never happened? You up in here fuckin' this bitch in our house and you want me to leave and act like it never happened?"

"Yeah, you heard me. You ain't had no business coming home early no way." My father looked past my mother into the bedroom where Betty was sitting up in bed and smoking a cigarette like it was her house. My mother tried to push past him in an attempt to get at her.

"You skanky bitch. You supposed to be my friend, bitch, and you up in here fuckin' my husband. Bitch, you 'bout to die!"

But my old man quickly cut those plans short. He hit my mother in the back of the head. When she fell to the floor in pain, he grabbed her by the back of her head and repeatedly punched her in the face with his fist. Betty looked on from the bedroom, laughing.

"You do what I tell you to do. This my house and I'll do what the fuck I please up in here. You got that?" He delivered a final backhand to her face before throwing her to the ground and looked at me with unforgiving eyes.

"You want some of this?"

I didn't move. I was so terrified that I pissed in my clothes. Henry walked back to the bedroom and closed the door behind him. I ran to my mother's side. She was crying and asking the Lord for strength.

She managed to pull herself off the floor though she was bleeding profusely. Her lip was split, her right eye was closed, and she had a small gash on her forehead.

"What do you want me to do, Momma?"

"There ain't nothing you can do, baby. I'll be okay." I got some ice out of the freezer and put it on her face. She stopped crying and stared at the bedroom door.

We could hear Betty and my father moving around,

talking and laughing. I held my mother's hand as she wiped the blood from her nose. About thirty minutes passed before the Rooster and Betty came out, fully dressed.

"I'll be back later on. Clean yourself up." He walked past my mother, holding his woman's hand. She winked at my mom and waved goodbye. I felt so sorry for my Momma though I was only nine years old and too little to understand everything that had just happened. But I knew I was tired of seeing my mother beaten up and hurt.

She ripped the sheets off the bed, dragged the mattress out of the house, and put it to the road. It wasn't the last time I would see her do that. Then she put the sheets into a plastic bag and threw them out too. She locked herself in the bedroom and I could hear her crying uncontrollably through the walls.

"Lord, please help me." That's all she would say between the tears.

. . . . .

Hours passed and I didn't hear my mother moving around or making noise. Suddenly I heard the front door open.

"Sylvia, where you at, baby?" My father had returned home. "Where you at, baby girl?" I could hear him walking through the house and opening closets because my mother often hid from him after he beat her up.

"I ain't mad at you, baby. I ain't mad that you put the mattress out. I know I was wrong. I just want to talk to you." He burst into my room with flowers in his hand.

"Where ya Momma?"

"I don't know. I thought she was in the room."

"Sylvia!" My father opened the linen closet. "Sylvia, come out now!"

I knocked on the bathroom door and tried to turn the knob but it was locked. "Daddy, I think she's in here."

"Move out the way." Henry banged on the door. "Open this door, baby girl. I said I was sorry and I bought you some pretty flowers."

There was no response and my father put his ear to the door. It was dead calm. So he threw himself against the door, breaking it down. "Oh Lord, what have you done? What have you done?"

My mother was in the tub, naked, and the water was red with blood. She had taken a hanger and shoved it up her vagina, killing the Rooster's child. "Oh Lawd . . . baby girl, why you do this? Why you do this?"

My father picked her up. She was pale from all the blood she'd lost. "Get me a blanket." I ran and got several blankets and he wrapped her up in them and walked quickly out to the car. "Open the door, boy. I want you to stay here. I got to go see about your momma. Go back into the house . . . go!"

They were gone for three days. Though I was only nine years old I was left alone to provide for myself.

I thought my father had taken my mother to the hospital but I later found out that he'd taken her to the root lady and she had nearly died having to depend on his country ass.

After they returned home my mother never looked or acted the same. She never went to church again. The Rooster was nice to us for a while but time passed, my mother got better, and he went back to being his old, ass-hole self.

But Henry wasn't the only one who made frequent trips to the root lady. My mother went often too. She didn't just do small things like spit in his food and bury his drawers in the yard. She took that whole voodoo shit to another level. I walked in the kitchen one evening and surprised my mother. She was preparing dinner for my father.

"Momma, why are you doing that?"

"Oh, it's nothing, baby." My mother pulled a steak out of her underwear. Apparently she had been wearing it between her legs. Her cycle was on and she had let her blood saturate the meat.

"Momma, why you doing that?" My mother looked at me.

"This something that I do for your father every now and then. This is our secret. You can't tell your father about this, okay?"

"Okay, but why are you doing it?"

"You wouldn't understand." My mother turned back to the counter and prepared the meat for my father. I looked on in disgust. Later that evening she placed Henry's plate down on the table.

"Why you not eating this good food your mother fixed?"

"I'm cool. I ate before you came home."

I looked at the steak with all the trimmings. My old man liked his steak rare and the blood from the half-cooked meat saturated the plate, spreading like a plague from the peas to the potatoes, and finally being soaked up by the bread. Henry devoured the meal. He often boasted how well my mother could cook.

"Baby girl, you put your foot in this," were his exact words. Little did he know that she had put more in it than her feet. After that day I never ate my mother's steak or spaghetti. I was a vegetarian until I moved out.

Order Additional Michael Gainer Titles:

Dumb As Me:
Women Gave Him Pleasure,
Misusing Them Gave Him More
ISBN: 0-9714887-0-3

One Life No Sequel:
Tomorrows Not Promised
ISBN: 0-9714887-1-1

Son Of A Rooster
The Prequel To *Dumb As Me*
ISBN: 0-9714887-2-X
(Coming Soon)